Co-Ed

HATE NEVER FELT SO TEMPTING

#1 NEW YORK TIMES BESTSELLING AUTHOR

RACHEL VAN DYKEN

Co-Ed
by Rachel Van Dyken

CO-ED
Copyright © 2018 RACHEL VAN DYKEN
IISBN-13: 9781682309728
Cover Art by Quirky Bird
Formatting by Jill Sava, Love Affair With Fiction

A Note From RVD

THE FIRST TIME I heard of the term reverse harem was actually a few years ago when I started the Eagle Elite Mafia series, there were four mob bosses basically all protecting and in love with one girl... because of that, I knew I wanted to take things a bit of a step further and write something where all the guys are a bit obsessed, a bit in love, but become good friends with the girl and the girl basically is only 'with' one guy. I know this term scares some people but it also excites some people, duh wouldn't it be fantastic to have a whole bunch of good looking guys chasing you around a college campus (in a totally healthy way mind you...)

This is my take on reverse harem, my fun way to add in a bit of sexy to a traditional college romance. I hope you like it!

HUGS, RVD

Dedication

To Nina,
thank you for being such a support and
encouragement.
I'm so happy to have you on my side ;)

Chapter One

Shawn

It started with a really loud moan, the kind that makes your body tingle and your senses so alert you could swear you actually hear the silence crackling around your face. Another moan sent my lazy heartbeat into a full-on thudding rhythm that sounded as if I'd been walking too aggressively across cement in high heels. It was so loud I was probably keeping my new roommate awake. Another moan followed. I sucked in a breath.

I'd been in this stupid dorm for two nights of pure hell, where I'd watched gross guy after gross guy put socks on their doors, followed by girls doing the walk of shame.

It wasn't my fault my name both looked and sounded like a guy's. Shawn is the name you hear a dad yell at a boy with a Yankees hat on while they play catch in the backyard—lucky for me, it was passed down the minute my mom got pregnant; they decided boy or girl, the name would be

Shawn. Sigh. That name came in handy most days. Except for the day they assigned me to the guys' dorm.

And transferring at the beginning of spring semester meant they literally had no other rooms for me.

It was this dorm…

Or homelessness.

Okay, not really. I could technically find a place, but that would mean rent I couldn't afford unless I found some other sad, unfortunate soul willing to live with me. And the thing about transferring to the University of Washington at the last minute in my junior year for softball? Well, that meant I had no other choice but to listen to the moaning.

Only this moan was different.

Really. Different.

The other moans had been sloppy, drunken.

This one sounded… nice.

Not that I ranked moans on a scale from one to ten.

But if I did, it would be a solid seven, maybe even an eight.

The moan was longer this time.

I shot up in my bed and listened.

"Go back to sleep." The gruff voice came from the other side of the room where my very male, and very metrosexual, roommate slept with a stuffed unicorn and a humidifier that made weird puffing noises because of his apparent dust allergies.

"Did you hear that?" I whispered.

He flipped over on his side, giving me a generous view of his six-pack and plaid pajama pants. I'd think he was attractive if he wasn't so bossy. The first day I unpacked my bags I had felt his judgement over everything I'd placed in my drawers, like they weren't folded well enough to deserve a spot.

"Everyone on the floor heard that. Seriously, sleep. You came here with dark circles under your eyes, and they're just going to get worse if you lay in your bed listening to the threesome across the way do their jobs."

My ears perked. "Threesome? Jobs?"

He put the white unicorn over his face and screamed into it.

What? Like I was the one being disruptive? I had practice at five in the morning! It was one in the morning; some of us needed uninterrupted sleep!

"Shawn." He said my name with a bit of disdain.

To be fair, he'd been open about the fact that he'd thought his new roommate was going to be less annoying than the last and, at the very least, packing a penis. I'd like to think he was right about the first and very irritated about the penis.

It's not my fault I was born a girl, right?

"Just try to go back to sleep. It's Friday, which means it's going to be a long night of moaning. If you need earplugs, I have spares in my desk."

"For situations like this?" *Seriously?*

"They give them out for free. Everyone knows it's necessary."

"Why the heck is it necessary?" My interest was more than piqued.

"Oh. My. Hell. What did I do? What? So I dumped her because she had a big middle toe! Everyone has their deal-breakers! Shit!" Slater threw his pillow onto the floor and stood, raking his hands through his hair, pacing like a madman.

Apparently, he had a thing about sleep, and apparently, I'd just made him irrationally angry over a breakup.

"So fucking what? Is this God's way of punishing me?" He looked up to the ceiling. "You give me a girl who can't even sleep through a few moans and doesn't even wash her face before bed? Kill me and get it over with!"

I gulped. "Hey, you okay?"

"No!" He glared over at me. "I'm not okay." The mocking air quotes gave it away. "I'm exhausted, and I need my sleep, and you talk more than my Aunt Gertrude who literally won't even stop talking during mass."

"Sorry?"

He inhaled deeply through his nostrils. "Look, I know you're curious — all the newbies are. I'm going to give you the short version, all right?"

"Um, okay." I sat up straighter.

He crooked his finger and walked over to the door that led to the living space separating us from their room.

I'd never seen a place so big and so nice at a university; again, another reason why I was still putting up with the moans.

Plus, it wasn't like Slater, my new roommate, was a slob.

He actually alphabetized his stuff.

And labeled all his products.

I slowly got up from the bed and walked over to where he stood by the door.

He looked up at me. "You're tall for a woman."

"You're short for a man," I fired back.

He just grinned. "Eh, maybe you aren't so bad. And I'm not short. I'm 5' 10". You're the monster here."

"Six foot. Big deal." I shrugged. Guys always had a problem with my height, but Slater seemed to be impressed by it, not intimidated. "So, what's the story?"

He opened the door a crack just as another moan rang

out. He bit down on his lip as three moans followed then a slight scream. "In three, two, one…"

The door across from us opened.

A beautiful girl stretched her arms over her head and cracked her neck. She was wearing jeans and a white crop top and had her dark, curly hair pulled up into a big ponytail. "Thanks guys. You always know how to work me."

I sucked in a breath just as Slater slapped a hand over my mouth. "Don't give us away. They don't like spies." His whisper was soft against my ear like he couldn't help but somehow sexualize everything.

"They? What? Like the Cold War's taking place in the space between us?" I rolled my eyes.

He didn't. "Watch."

A tall guy with lazy green eyes and a man bun stepped out and crossed his arms. His skinny jeans rode so low on his hips it was almost indecent, and of course, he had no shirt on.

So… they were having sex?

Another guy stepped out. He had blond hair, killer abs, same outfit, like it was a uniform or something, as another guy followed him out. He was the one that made my heart do a weird thud. He was tall. Really tall. At least 6' 6", with more muscles than I knew existed on another human and a deadly smile that looked slightly crooked; and, of course, one small dimple dented the right side of his mouth, and blond locks hung past his ears. Were they all descendants of Thor or something? Trying out for *Vikings? Game of Thrones?* Where did an individual find that many good-looking men? And what monster would put them in the same room together?

The last guy looked like Charlie Hunnam and Brad Pitt had gotten it on and somehow had a baby. I almost couldn't look away.

"They have that effect on all their clients," Slater whispered.

He was still there? I hadn't noticed.

"And before you start lusting, remember, they don't date. They… please."

"Come again?" I whispered.

"Oh, they do, and often." What a stupid response. "Although they do have this ironclad, no intercourse rule, but last year rumor had it that three girls orgasmed by one of the guys holding a box of Cheerios."

"Shut up!" I hissed.

Slater held up his hands. "Don't shoot the messenger."

"So, they… please girls." I licked my lips. *Disgusting. Who made a job out of that? And three of them? Wasn't that awkward?*

One of them, the blond Viking-looking sexy one, bent down and kissed the side of the girl's neck while the other two flanked each side. They all touched her intimately, but not in a way that was overtly sexual, almost as if they just wanted to show her they were close — oh, and you know — shared an insane amount of body heat.

She closed her eyes, and her head fell back while the tall one tilted her chin toward him and whispered, "Make sure you hydrate and text us if you need anything else."

She slipped something into his hands and, honest to God, stumbled toward the door like she'd just been drugged.

It clicked shut.

Slater put his forefinger on my chin and shut my gaping mouth just as all three of them looked across the room and smiled.

I should have dodged those smiles. Should have slammed

the door in disgust. Instead, I was so damn intrigued I opened it wider and glared.

"No, no! They like a challenge, don't just—" Slater was already pulling me back.

I crossed my arms and stared them down.

Before I realized I was in nothing but a sports bra and a see-through tank top.

They looked their fill, their expressions varying degrees of leer.

Tropical-quality heat swamped me.

Finally, Slater was able to pull me back into our room. He slammed the door shut behind him and locked it for good measure. "Stay. Away."

I gave my head a shake. "Trust me, I'm not into sharing, and I don't date during the season."

He scoffed. "They don't date either, and they have loads of rules. I've seen them convert a girl destined for the convent, so you can see why I'm concerned that your pulse just picked up."

"It did not!" I gulped. The warmth that had flooded my body slowly dissipated.

He pressed his hand to my neck and swore. "Don't lie to your new roommate. It's rude."

I slapped his hand away. "I thought you hated me because I have boobs."

"Oh, I love boobs." He grinned widely. "I just don't want yours. I'm not into taller girls, or ones who happen to be my roommate when I specifically asked for a quiet athlete whose cleanliness was better than Steve's." He shrugged.

"Steve?"

"All Steves are dirty. Registrar should just know these things. Steve used to clip his toenails onto the floor — just sprinkled them around like fairy dust. And don't even get me started on CrossFit Steve's calluses and his joy in ripping them off and showing me just how big one chunk of skin could be. Oh right, and he typically did this before dinner. How else do you think I got the abs?"

I snorted out a laugh. "So, CrossFit Steve's both your curse and your inspiration?"

I could have sworn his eye twitched before he gave his head a shake. "I can tell you're one of the good ones. Don't fall for it. Stay far, far, far away. In fact, you should move." He eyed me up and down. "How do you feel about Siberia?"

I walked back to my bed. "I'm not moving to Siberia because I'm living in the same dorm with some weird co-eds who like to please women."

"Women, men, plants... my grandma. They'll do it all for a price, and often, together. Just... stay away."

He moved back to his bed and pulled the duvet over his face. I heard a muffled sigh as he threw it back off his body and stared me down. "I mean it. The Pleasure Ponies are bad news."

I burst out laughing. "Please tell me that's their real name!"

He joined in. "Nah, that's my nice nickname for them. The real company name is under Wingman, Inc."

I stilled. "The matchmaking company that Facebook tried to buy out last year?"

He nodded. "Both gurus wanted to leave a legacy. Handpicked those three to work for them here at the University. When one graduates, another's nominated, and let's just put it this way... Those guys? Raking it in... no shame whatsoever."

"But how? Why?"

He yawned. "Because we live in a world full of broken hearts, and everyone wants to be told the lie."

I felt small. I wanted to crawl into my bed and cry a bit. "What lie?"

"That it's not you. It's them. That the world will give you better, that you'll get your happily ever after, that life is like the movies — that we don't live in a sea full of broken, fucked up hearts."

We stopped talking after that.

I lay awake for two more hours wondering if he could see my insecurity, my pain.

And pondering how I was going to hide it from the ones who promised to fix it — for a price.

Chapter Two

Shawn

I woke up feeling like death, with my new bestie holding some weird-looking moisturizer over my head — more like, hovering it over me in hopes that the movement would take away my black circles. I slapped his hand away.

It just came back.

"Resistance is futile," he quipped, pumping some into his smooth perfect-looking tan hands and trying to slap it on my face.

"Stop that!" I tried to move his hands away, but he was stronger than he looked. "Seriously, I haven't even washed my face yet. What's with you?"

He sighed as if he was disappointed in both me and life. "This is face wash — well, it's a mask and a wash, but you look like hell, and I can't have people knowing you're my roommate if you leave in your current state. It will completely destroy my reputation. Plus, I feel sorry for your face — I really do. You look rough. Did you even sleep last night?"

I glared. Too many questions. Not enough coffee. "I'm not your project."

He was silent for a moment then said, "You sure?" He reached for a mirror.

"Don't," I warned again, clenching my teeth.

He just shrugged. "I can't have your dark circles on my conscience. I'll get hives. Do you want me to get hives?"

"Is this a trick question?"

"Holy shit! You want me to break out in hives this close to the holidays? Unbelievable!" He looked up to the ceiling again. "Her feet smelled, all right? They were big, and they were smelly and cold. I don't do cold!"

"Who you talking to, big fella?" I smirked.

He glared down at me then slapped the gunk into my hand. "Three minutes. Don't wash until it feels itchy, follow with number three, then four, and then yes, you can moisturize." He pointed to the sink. "They're all labeled. I take it you know how to pump stuff into your hands?"

"You sure you're into boobs?" I smiled and earned a pillow and the unicorn thrown in my direction.

"I model. It's necessary, and no, that wasn't an open-ended statement where you get to give me your opinion or ask questions. And in case you care, I had acne when I was a teen — and exactly one friend who I named Fred because he wasn't actually real, and you can name your invisible friends anything."

"Tell me you have friends now."

His toothy grin would be gorgeous if he wasn't so annoying. "Loads, but I don't talk much when I'm with my friends."

"Ah, too busy using your tongue?"

"Waste it on words or on a woman? Let me think about it."

"Gross." I stood and stretched my arms over my head. "You know, you could be one of those Pleasure Ponies."

"Not into sharing," he said quickly. "And all three of them are really good at it. I'm serious. Far away, Shawn. It's the least I can do."

"Oh?"

His smile deepened. "But start clipping your toenails out in the open, and I'll probably zip tie you to a rolling chair and send you sailing toward their door."

"Petty threat." I grabbed my towel and shower caddy, gave him a two-fingered wave, and slipped my flip-flops on. I had exactly twenty minutes to get ready, and I couldn't stop yawning.

The lights were already on when I walked into the bathroom. At least this floor was co-ed; they just meant for girls to be in a suite together, not one shared with four guys, but whatever. Again, being stuck with Slater, I wasn't going to complain.

Plus, I had to admit, with a shrug, whatever he was trying to dump on my face smelled really good. My flip-flops squeaked against the tile floor. One shower was running, but the other ten were open. I rounded the corner and turned on my Spotify playlist to wake me up. Chainsmokers started blaring as I grabbed my blue towel, placed it on the hook near the curtain, and adjusted the water to searing hot.

I was just pulling my sports bra over my head when the water in the shower a few stalls down turned off.

I glanced to my left. Not that I wanted to see a naked girl; it was just instinct to check.

What I saw was not boob.

Or soft.

Or anything feminine whatsoever.

It was one of the Ponies.

I quickly looked away as if I'd just been caught doing something wrong, but I knew he saw me, knew I hadn't been quick enough.

Perfect dilemma.

Did I keep stripping and just jump into the shower? Or wait for him to leave? But if I waited, I would look nervous, or maybe like I was trying to talk to him.

My upper lip was starting to sweat as steam billowed out of the shower in front of me.

With jerky movements, I pulled off my shorts then my underwear and dove into the shower, ready to wrap the curtain around my naked body if need be.

After a few seconds of heavy breathing on my part, I let out a rough exhale and was about to reach for my caddy when a masculine hand shot out from the curtain and handed me my lavender body wash.

"Uh, thanks, man." I jerked it away from him, only to have that stupid attractive hand reappear and hand me my loofah. "Thanks... again."

"No problem."

My body swayed, the universe tilted, and I felt my thighs quiver. This was bad. So bad. It was just my overactive imagination. His voice didn't really sound like warm velvet with a hint of just enough rasp to make me want to lean in and see if it felt funny against my neck.

Nope.

Not at all.

I didn't realize how vigorously I was scrubbing until the skin on my arms started tingling, and when I glanced at it, saw it turning red.

I tried calming down, mentally going to a different place, just as the shower curtain was pulled aside and, let's just call him Pony Number One, leaned against the wall, towel wrapped low on his hips and arms crossed.

He didn't once look at my breasts.

No, his focus was only on my face, which actually made it more uncomfortable. I wanted a reason to slap him, to shove him away, to tell him he was being a creeper.

Instead, he was looking into my eyes with such intensity I forgot to breathe and started choking a bit before I hissed, "Did you need something?"

"No," he said politely. "But thanks for asking."

The shower curtain was still open, and my teeth started to chatter.

Without looking away from my eyes, his hand reached for the handle, and the water grew hotter.

"Uh, thanks," I mumbled.

What game was he playing?

Why hadn't Slater told me more? Were there specific rules I had to follow? Was this guy expecting me to pay him for making my water hot and handing me body wash?

Oh, no!

He was, wasn't he?

That's what they did!

They pleased women!

"I don't have cash on me," I blurted in the least sexy voice you could possibly imagine all breathy and squeaky like I'd just swallowed my own body wash.

He threw his head back and laughed. "Oh, this may be the best day of my life."

God, his voice was beautiful. Like the string section of

a symphony orchestra, smooth and mellow. I wanted to ask him to say something else. Already, I was leaning in without even realizing it. I jerked back and almost collided with the tile behind me.

"Oh?" I was already knee-deep in my own embarrassment. *Why not take the plunge?*

He moved closer, until drops of moisture hit his perfect jawline. The steam billowed around both of our heads, and I could smell the Irish Spring he must have just slathered all over that perfect body. Instantly, I wanted to run to the store and buy a case and open every wrapper until my room filled with his scent.

"You don't need to tip me for being a gentleman." He grinned wider, and my tongue turned to sandpaper. "Though, out of curiosity, what do you think a nice rubdown would get me, hmm?"

He wasn't—

He wouldn't, would he?

He ran one finger…

One. Finger.

…down my shoulder until it collided with my elbow. The air backed up in my lungs. Every muscle in my body tensed, and as that finger ran back up, I melted. My legs turned to jelly. How was that reaction even possible? I still felt his stupid finger's presence as he licked his lips and whispered, "Nice meeting you, Shawn."

Then he was gone.

Dumbfounded, I just shouted, "I didn't tell you my name!"

"I know!" he called back with a chuckle, leaving my entire body on fire and my left eye twitching as I stared straight ahead at the blue tile. *What the hell had just happened?*

It must have been all over my face, because by the time I made it back into the room, Slater took one look at me and swore.

"What did I tell you?" He jerked me inside, slammed the door behind us, and braced his body against it like Pony Number One was going to come at it with a battering ram. "Don't challenge them!"

"I was in a shower!" I poked him in the chest. "He, he, he—"

"Oh hell, you're already stuttering, and he probably just said, 'Hi.' Am I right?"

Heat flooded my cheeks, and I didn't blush often. Thanks to my father's African American heritage, my skin was always a perfect olive tone, making it impossible to see a bright blush.

Until now.

Until the Ponies.

I cleared my throat. "I was naked, he poked his head in the shower, peeled back the curtain, gave me my freaking body wash, and then I didn't know what to do."

Slater's lips twitched. "Um, how about you knee him in the balls and say, 'Get the hell out, you asshole'?"

"Right." I nodded. "I was about to, but I was embarrassed. You know, what if he was doing it for a… tip?" I gulped. The more I spoke the hotter my cheeks felt.

Slater's eyes widened before he burst out laughing and wiped a tear from his eye. "Please tell me you offered to pay him. Please. It would make my entire year of suffering with toenail clippings worth it."

"I just…" I glared, silently willing an asteroid to drop on his pretty face. "I told him I didn't have cash."

Slater braced his body against the door, shaking with

laughter like it was the funniest thing he'd ever heard in his entire life.

"It's not that funny." I quickly grabbed his stupid moisturizer from the counter, slathered it on, and pulled a hoodie over my head. "And I need to get to practice."

He was still laughing when I jerked the door open and looked down. My mortification was complete. A twenty-dollar bill was on the floor, with a yellow sticky note message stuck to it.

I know my own worth. For next time.
Love, Leo.

Slater looked over my shoulder and snorted. "At least it was Leo. He's more… house broke than the others. I don't think the guy's ever even been in a serious relationship, or would even know what it was if it was living with him." He bent over and snatched up the twenty then handed it to me. "That's at least three coffee runs, and all because he saw you naked. Sounds like a win to me."

I tossed the money back at Slater and turned on my heel just in time to see Leo poke his head out of his room. "Was it good for you?"

I flipped him off and slammed the door behind me, ignoring the way my lungs grappled with air, and the way my entire body still buzzed with the way his one stupid finger had felt running down my arm.

Chapter Three

Shawn

I MADE IT to the weight room just in time to see that I was about four minutes late. Coach Jackson didn't even lift his head from the clipboard as he pointed at the wall.

With a grumble, I marched over to the wall, grabbed the twenty-five-pound weight, and slid down, adding the weight to my knees when I was at the perfect forty-five-degree angle.

Lucky for me, one of my teammates was another two minutes behind me. I looked closer; something about her appeared... off. She rubbed her runny nose against her team sweatshirt, grabbed a weight, and joined me.

"Everything okay?" I asked. My thighs burned so badly I wanted to scream. I was only forty-five seconds in; three minutes fifteen seconds to go!

"My boyfriend broke up with me," Alexa muttered. "He said I wasn't spending enough time with him. I wasn't feeding his needs."

"Feed this." I flipped off the air.

She laughed and wiped at another tear as she sank down next to me. "He's an ass. All men are asses. They should all burn!"

Coach Jackson eyed us and cleared his throat; he wanted us to know he was listening to our conversation.

I lowered my voice. "So…" Why was I still hung up on these guys? "…I know I just transferred, but I heard about these guys who—"

"No-o-o…" Alexa shook her head. "I couldn't. Do you even know the reputation those guys have? Girls get so hung up on them it's like an addiction. No joke. I know a girl who works an extra shift every week just so she gets one hour with the guys."

I shrugged. "One extra shift? That's not that bad."

Alexa snorted. "The woman cans sardines at the fishery, on her feet, in the dark, smelling like fish. Yeah, it is that bad — trust me — but to her, totally worth it. You should see her drugged-up face when she comes back. Rumor has it they use drugs to keep people coming back, but they swear everything they do is legal."

"My ass," I teased, though every part of me had felt drugged by one fingertip, so who was I to judge? Slater was right. *Stay away. Far, far, away.*

"Anyway…" she shrugged. "…I'll just get over it the old-fashioned way."

"Darcy, chocolate, and ice cream?"

"Hell, yes!"

My muscles screamed accusations of physical trauma, and I started to wince as my last fifteen seconds rolled around.

I dropped to the floor as soon as I could and slammed the plate against the rubber mat, giving my coach a dirty look while he was turned.

"Saw that, McKenzie," he yelled.

I just groaned and started to stretch.

I had a lot of warming up to do.

And a lot of pain to endure if I was going to stop thinking about the guys across the living space. Besides, our games didn't start for another month, and during that month I'd be working my ass off trying to build muscle, get into shape, and not flunking out of Human Anatomy.

"Squats!" Coach blew the whistle, much to the dismay of every woman in the room.

I stood on wobbly legs and realized it had completely worked.

Exercise had taken my mind off the Ponies.

And the embarrassing shower situation. Besides, it was not like I would see a lot of them, since they did all of their business in their room.

I shuddered.

Drugs. It had to be illegal drugs.

"So…" Alexa fell in stride next to me as we walked over to one of the coffee shops to grab some food. "…you got a boyfriend?"

I rolled my eyes. "Between sports, school, and trying to find a part-time job, when would I even have time?"

"You're telling me," she sighed, and I could tell she was sad; she was even walking like she was trying out for the part of Eeyore.

"Look." I opened the door to the shop and let her in. Warm air immediately comforted the chill on my arms. "He wasn't your lobster — that's all you gotta worry about. True lobsters stay together forever, and it sounds like he was more worried about himself than you."

She blinked away another tear.

"Why don't you come over tonight? We can watch a few movies? I'll even order pizza or something."

Alexa sniffled. "Why are you being so nice to me? You don't even know me."

"Single ladies have to stick together." I winked. "Besides, I'm new, and it would be good to have a friend who isn't my male roommate."

She frowned, confusion registering in her eyes. "Wait, how did that happen?"

"Long story."

"Tell it, and I'll pay for our drinks."

"Deal." I smiled as we both put in our orders.

Alexa went to the bathroom while I found a seat by the window.

I was just starting to dig into my bacon gouda sandwich when I smelled it.

Or him.

Not really an *it*.

Aftershave that held the hint of rain and cedar mixed with mint, and something so damn sexy I had no choice but to look up. I was suddenly lucky I hadn't taken a bite. I would have choked, he would have saved my life, and I would have still died of mortification.

"This seat taken?" It was one of the Pleasure Ponies. Yeah, I wasn't going to survive one day if they kept pestering me.

I cleared my throat. It was one of the guys who'd come

out of the room first. Not the one who was scary attractive. On a scale of one to ten, would I sell my parents for this guy? No. Would I send them to Siberia for a year and let him kiss me in every secret place?

Yes.

So, yeah, on the hot scale? Still pretty damn hot.

"Yes," I finally spoke up. His chocolate eyes crinkled at the sides as he ran a muscled hand — yes, even his hand had muscle — through his cropped, honey-blond hair.

"Really?" He leaned those same hands against the table, casting a shadow over me with his massive body.

The aftershave hit harder. *A hundred bucks says they discovered a way to put crack in cologne and were selling it on the black market.*

"No, I'm lying," I said with a straight face. "Yes, really."

"I'm Finn."

He didn't hold out his hand.

So I didn't offer mine. "That's nice."

He bit down on his lower lip, showing me nice white teeth from a smile that would make a whore turn in her own pimp. "You live across from us, right? The girl with the pretty hair."

Aw, he'd said my hair was pretty! My heart might have stuttered bit as I mentally did a hair flip and winked like I had game — which I didn't.

Calm down! Focus!

Mental slap.

And another one for good measure.

I smiled. "That's me."

"With the guy's name?"

"Like Finn is any better?" I said sarcastically. "Is it even short for anything, or were your parents just not very creative?"

"Finneas Arthur Titus." His grin widened. "The third."

I felt a bit weak in the stomach. The Titus family was known throughout the entire Pacific Northwest. If Seattle had royalty, they would be it.

"How nice for you, Finneas Arthur Titus, the third." I tried not to look impressed.

He just threw his head back and laughed. "Knox was right. We really should stay away from you."

My ears perked. Where was Alexa? How long did it take to pee? "Knox?"

"The hot one," he said in a serious tone.

"What's that make you? The ugly one?" I fired back.

"Oh, I'm the sexy one," he said, completely deadpan. "Leo's the sensitive one, and Knox? Well, he's the one everyone just wants to fuck. But he doesn't like playing with his food, so…"

"You're a douchebag." There. I'd said it.

"Thank you." He put his hand on his heart just as Alexa approached.

"It's like they don't understand the concept of flushing! Just flush the damn tampon and be done with it— Oh, hello th-th-there." She finally got it out on the third try and gave me a withering look.

"Alexa Hampton." Did he know everyone's name? Was he a child genius or something? "It's a pleasure."

My eye felt twitchy as he reached for her hand, kissed the back of it, and winked.

"Alrighty then." I moved to grab my coffee and food. "We were just going, so if you'll just return to the 1800s…" I had to physically help Alexa stand. Even then I was worried she was already under his spell as she stumbled with me out the door.

When I turned around, Finn was still staring.

He blew me a kiss.

It made my knees weak, while at the same time, forced me to wonder if the guys had found a new target, a new challenge, a plaything who would entertain their bored, rich minds.

Not this bitch!

"How do you know him?" Alexa finally found words ten minutes later.

"I don't," I said truthfully.

She stopped walking. "They don't just approach people, not in public at least. One time a girl tried talking to Finn in line at the Apple store, and he straight-up ignored her for twenty minutes. She tried again a day later, and his eyes glazed over as he said, *'Who are you?'*"

Ouch, that had to have hurt. I winced. "That's rough."

"Rough?" Alexa repeated. "She was devastated."

"How do they stay in business?" I wondered out loud.

"I'm telling you, drugs!" she hissed. "Okay, I need to go to class. I'll see you tonight!"

I didn't have the heart to tell her that I lived across the suite from them, or that we'd have to lock our door, just in case.

Yeah, I was so going to have to buy a rape horn or something irritating. It was the only way to keep my head sane.

And my heart safe.

Chapter Four

Knox

"Wʜᴀᴛ ᴀʀᴇ ʏᴏᴜ two dipshits doing?" I was bored as fuck, going through our schedule for the next two weeks. Same girl, same girl, same girl, same guy, same grandma — *the hell? I thought she died?* I shook my head; it didn't help with the pulsing or the boredom. Four more months and I was out of this place; four more months and I could focus on my internship with Wingman, Inc.

They'd trusted me with this.

And I was going to see it through.

I busted my ass for that company, made an insane salary, and was being groomed all through college for a future job. I just had to suffer a little while longer.

A text came through.

Unknown: *I'll pay you five hundred dollars for a nude shot.*

Me: *Lose this number. That's not what this business is about.*

Unknown: *A thousand.*

I groaned and tossed my phone onto the desk; I pressed my palms against my head in an effort to get the ache to go away.

"Guys?" *Did they leave?*

They were taking turns spying on God knows what in the shared living room. I finally got up and shoved them out of the way, pulled the door open, and scowled.

There she was.

The girl from last night.

The one both guys wouldn't shut up about.

Apparently, she was walking, talking sex with wild hair, olive skin, and a banging body. And according to Leo, breasts that he wanted to die between.

I wasn't interested.

I was actually surprised they were.

They didn't date. They did their damn jobs day in and day out, and when they wanted sex, they went off campus. We didn't mix business with pleasure.

Ever.

Her light brown eyes locked with mine.

I grunted.

Then slammed the door not quite hard enough to bring it off the hinges.

"What the hell, man?" Finn laughed. "You trying to scare her away?"

"No," I said through my gritted teeth. "I think that was all Leo this morning during shower time."

Leo just laughed. "You should have seen her strip. So

fast, I'm surprised she didn't chip a tooth against the tile and end up ass backwards with her feet in the air. So damn cute." His face fell. "Sometimes I miss it, the innocent ones."

"They *are* all innocent," Finn piped up. "Honestly, we're the ones who ruin them."

"Shut the hell up!" Leo snapped. "And any girl who pays us to massage her while we brush her hair and talk about My Little Pony is hella innocent."

I shuddered. She was our regular. And she terrified me. One of us brushed her hair, one massaged, and one held the pony.

Fucking. Weird.

But she paid well, and that was our job. *Wasn't it?*

Always please.

Never penetrate.

Holy shit, what kind of hell hole am I in?

I didn't realize I was groaning out loud until Leo tossed me a pillow and said, "Just in case you need to get a good scream in."

I caught it midair then slammed it against the floor. "I don't need to scream. I need this semester to be over."

Finn grinned stupidly. "I know what's wrong."

"We're paid escorts who don't get to have sex?" I said out loud. "People think we're selling drugs? Or how about the last dude that came up in here that thought we were going to offer a ménage?"

"Hey, at least he was attractive." Leo shrugged. "And people always to get the wrong idea about us. So what? We make bank, and for the most part every customer leaves happy, satisfied, and dreaming about the next time they can sign over hundreds of dollars to spend time in our company."

It wasn't that it felt wrong.

I was just tired of doing the grunt work.

I was tired of pretending.

"You need to get laid," Leo said quietly. "Too much touching, not enough boinking."

"Say 'boinking' again, and I'm not speaking to you for a month," I grumbled.

Finn just shrugged and pointed. "What about new girl across the way? She's beautiful. I think it's been established that her breasts are fluffy pillows of ecstasy, and she's funny — double bonus."

"Breasts and comedy? Gee, where do I sign up?" I said in a sarcastic voice.

"The hell?" Finn shook his head. "Did you just say, 'gee'?"

I gave him the finger and stood.

"And Leo has a point. Just get in and out, maybe twice. First time will be too quick anyway since it's been a while—"

I growled.

"Then you'll have that winning attitude on lockdown."

"Be honest. I've never had a winning attitude," I whispered under my breath.

They fell silent.

Shit. I'd done it again.

Mentioned what I swore we would never talk about.

Any of us.

We'd been friends since freshman year. I'd recruited them after the masterminds behind the Pacific Northwest's biggest dating service recruited me, and the rest was history.

Money had started piling in. Who knew how many broken hearts existed in our sad pathetic world? And let's just say, lucrative was an understatement.

The sound of the communal microwave went off as the smell of something burning filled the air. I was out of the room before anyone could stop me and stomping over to the microwave with loud, purposeful steps that probably sounded, to the people a floor below us, like an elephant was going for a run.

I jerked the popcorn out of the microwave and cursed just as the girl — fine, I knew her name — just as Shawn ran out of her room and gasped.

I dangled it in the space between us as my completely unamused expression stared down her embarrassed one, and I bet my soul, and hers, that Finn and Leo were watching the entire exchange.

Hell, they were probably taking bets.

I tilted my head. "This yours?"

She hesitated, giving me time to take in her short, black sleep shorts and almost nonexistent white tank top. At least she was wearing a bra, though it just made the whole situation worse since it was pushing her tits together like they wanted to invite someone in for a good time. "Yes."

"Just, yes?"

She frowned. "Yes, that's my popcorn?"

"This isn't popcorn. It's not even edible." I gave the bag a shake. "Do you really think you should be in college if you can't even work a microwave?"

Her face fell then she scowled. "I refuse to be insulted by some guy who has longer hair than me and clearly has a scissor phobia."

Stunned, I just stared her down. "I'd be very careful what comes next out of that mouth of yours."

She grinned, stuck out a pink tongue that had my entire body tightening then sauntered over to me, grabbed the burnt popcorn, opened the damn bag, and said, "Thanks for your help. Next time I'll be sure to share."

It wasn't as burnt as I'd thought.

Was it edible? No.

Was she? Hell, yes, and my body was already chiming in on that fact. Blood thundered through my veins, sending every ounce of strength south.

I crossed my arms and leaned in. "Oh, I'm all about sharing."

"Clearly." She eyed my door.

I refused to turn around.

"I bet you're very giving…"

"Care to find out?" I moved closer. What the hell was I doing? It was like my mouth had taken control of my body, and my body was cheering it on while my brain just rolled over and died.

Her eyes fell to my lips then slowly she looked her fill, from my feet all the way back up. Her chest rose and fell. I knew that look. Her heart was racing, her thighs quivering. Ten seconds. I could get her off in ten seconds. Maybe six.

"Nah." She finally shrugged. "I think I'll just stick to my popcorn and Netflix."

"Hurry the hell up!" Slater yelled from the room then opened the door, took in our exchange, and paled. "Shawn… back away from the man whore… slowly. If you walk too fast, they take it as a challenge and pounce."

"Bite me!" I snapped at him.

Someone I used to call friend.

Someone I didn't want to see but had no choice to communicate with since we'd been wrongly placed in the same college suite in the same dorm.

He flipped me off.

I was too focused on Slater to notice that Shawn had actually listened to the dipshit and was already safely back in her room.

The door clicked shut.

I heard Leo's low whistle first, followed by Finn's slow clap. I turned and glared. I had no words. Maybe it was the pounding headache, but I'd never been turned down by a woman, man — human. They all wanted me, or something from me. So, I was about as angry as I was confused and in utter shock that she'd just turned around and walked away as if I wasn't everyone's perfect brand of drug.

"Shit, you look more confused than Finn does in Human Anatomy," Leo mused while Finn rolled his eyes. "Did she just... reject the great Knox Tate?"

"Maybe she was busy," Finn added.

"Washing her hair?" Leo snorted with laughter while I wondered how much trouble I would get into if I pushed them out the three-story windows in our shared dorm room.

"Forget it." I stomped past them and went back to work, back to the texts, back to the schedule.

Back to my own personal hell.

Chapter Five

Shawn

I WAS EATING burnt popcorn. Drinking lukewarm Diet Coke.

And dreaming about the ice in the freezer that I refused to walk back to, especially if the tall one was standing there guarding it like a prison guard.

I chomped harder on the popcorn and must have growled or something because Alexa started giving me a side-eye as if I was the problem, when everything wrong with the universe was living across the shared space.

"Taking out your frustration on the popcorn?" she asked.

I stopped chewing and stared at the TV. What were we even watching? I literally had to mentally backtrack to our conversation about Marvel versus DC before it registered that it was Thor in front of me.

Which didn't help the situation.

Thor had long hair.

Hot, rude guy had long hair.

It was a serious problem.

Made worse by the fact that he and Slater seemed to have some sort of beef that made my entire room smell like testosterone. I could actually feel his man-juices getting pissed off and swirly inside his body. He also kept punching his stuffed unicorn every few seconds.

"And here I thought you guys were supposed to be cheering me up." Alexa blew out an exasperated breath. "All men suck, burn, burn, burn…" She elbowed me and laughed while Slater stopped punching the unicorn long enough to stare at the two of us with heavy skepticism.

"So…" I cleared my throat. "…you and the tall one? Used to be… friends?" I guessed.

"Lovers?" Alexa just had to add.

I tossed a piece of popcorn at her face while Slater groaned and moved to a sitting position.

His six-pack was in full view. He clearly had something against clothing; he was in nothing but a pair of black jogger pants and a Nike beanie. Pieces of his caramel-colored hair were plastered against his forehead and tucked behind his ears, making him look younger.

"How does, 'I don't want to talk about it' sound?" He cracked his knuckles. "And do I really look gay? He wasn't my lover."

"Ri-i-ght." Alexa nodded. "Says the guy with enough face products to open up his own Sephora. I totally believe you, though." She winked slowly.

He gritted his teeth. "I like women—" He stopped then eyed her up and down. "—not that you would know if one hit you upside the head, but do you even own a brush?"

She glared. "Why? Are you offering to give me your

favorite horsehair one? I've heard it makes things really shiny."

"Shiny, my ass!" Slater ground out through his teeth.

"Guys…" I stood, ready to separate them. "…play nice."

"I would if we had popcorn that wasn't burnt — and ice, the crushed kind." Alexa frowned into her cup. "Why are we trapped in the room again?"

"Because…" I crossed my arms and swallowed hard then shared a knowing look with Slater. "…the tall one…" I left out the hot part. "…was offering to share… things…" I gulped. "…and we don't do things like that."

"Good girls go bad…" Slater started to sing then hummed the rest.

I grabbed his unicorn and tossed it at his face.

He caught it just in time.

"Fine. You want ice?" I jerked open the door and whispered in a low voice, "I'll get the damn ice."

"You go girl." Alexa whistled. "You get yours!"

"Shhhh!" Slater cupped a hand over her mouth. "Do you want them to hear? They'll think she wants some, actual *some*, not ice."

Alexa just shrugged. "Shouldn't one of us be getting sex?"

"Huh, woman has a point, but they don't do sex, so… I guess nothing to worry about."

I frowned then turned back around and shut the door behind me. "What do they really do then? The moans we heard Friday meant sex, or what? Do they just control the energy field around a woman's body?"

Slater rolled his eyes. "All pleasure, no penetration. It's their slogan."

I gasped. "What douchebags!"

Alexa burst out laughing. "Ah, I feel better already…

Who uses that as a slogan?"

"They do." Slater broke eye contact then scratched his head. "So where are we on the ice situation?"

I wasn't sure.

About anything.

Ice.

Life.

The universe's obvious hatred of me for putting three guys across the living room who decided it would be fun to toy with my emotions and touch me and…

Chapter Six

Knox

"SHE'S BACK," LEO whispered.

I pretended not to hear him.

Finn threw a pencil at my face.

I dodged it and added in another client for the following night — one of the normal ones who'd recently been dumped by her fiancé and just wanted to talk. I rubbed her feet, Leo gave a killer hand massage, and since Finn was a talker, he sat in front of her and said things like, *"I understand, tell me more. All men should burn. You're really pretty when you cry. Aw shit, did I say too much?"*

It used to feel good.

Making them feel good.

Now it just felt like I was lying through my ass every time someone paid us to make them feel better. We were untrained therapists with too much charm; it was a damn dangerous problem to have.

"Ice, ice, baby…" Finn started singing then stood. "I think I'll go get some…"

"Some." Leo grinned. "You know what? I'm suddenly parched as well. Knox? Care to join us?"

I grunted.

And eventually caved by way of peer pressure and a shit ton of jealousy that they were going to be able to get close enough to smell her skin. *What the hell was that? Lavender?* I stood, praying to God she'd at least put on a baggy sweatshirt that hid her perfectly rounded tits.

Leo was out first, followed by Finn. It was how these things worked. We always sent Leo in first because the last time we all approached a woman at the same time, we'd had to call the paramedics; it had been a panic attack, not a heart attack, but it had freaked us out enough to make sure we didn't just intimidate the hell out of whoever we were supposed to be sucking up to.

"Shower Girl…" Leo rubbed his hands together while I leaned against the farthest wall away from them. He towered over her, every muscle in his body tight. I didn't miss the way she looked at his biceps like they were an ice cream cone, and he was offering her unlimited licks. He wore T-shirts for that very reason, and skinny jeans to show off his tight ass. Can't make this shit up.

I waited while she gulped and tried to sidestep him.

It was amusing watching her inward struggle.

And I felt like an ass for wanting to join in the teasing just to see how far I could push her before she screamed my name and crawled back for more. It had been a while since I'd developed any sort of interest in someone of the opposite sex who wasn't part of my job.

I would never admit it.

But maybe they were right.

"Hold up." Leo reached out and grazed a finger down her arm as he cornered her. "You should moisturize after showering. It's one of the rules of living in a dry environment."

"We live in Seattle." She crossed her arms.

Leo grinned. "I meant the dorms, but thanks for the geography lesson. I've always had a very serious teacher-student fantasy, and you just brought a sliver of that to life." He leaned down until his face was inches from hers.

Her breaths came in small gasps. Her eyes were wide.

"I wouldn't be a gentleman if I didn't give you a proper thank you."

Her eyes went from horrified to insulted as she really did sidestep him, grabbed two glasses from the cupboard, and attempted to get ice out of the freezer.

"Here, let me." Finn trapped her on the other side, grabbed both glasses from her hands, and filled them up with ice then handed them back.

It was classic Wingman style.

Good cop, bad cop.

Compliment her, come on to her then the next guy sweeps in to make her feel like he was the safer choice, the guy next door. That was Finn. I knew what was next.

Showtime.

Slowly, I approached the three of them.

"What are you guys watching?" Finn asked, crossing his arms and leaning a safe two feet away from her, commanding her attention while Leo slowly braced behind her and started running his hands down her arms as if she was shivering.

Then she really did shiver. "You guys are bad news."

"No," Finn scoffed, "we're the good ones. I can promise you that."

"Well, the good ones are touching me," she pointed out.

Leo laughed and stopped rubbing. "You looked cold."

"I'm not."

"So, would you say you're hot then?" Finn asked.

"Why does this feel like a trap?" she wondered out loud, glancing at the full cups in her hands. "If I answer right, can I go back to my room?"

"Why would you want to do that?" Leo said from behind her. "I promise you'll have more fun out here."

"Yes, having an orgy sounds awesome," she deadpanned.

Finn burst out laughing. "Honey, I'm sure it would be, but that's not exactly what goes on behind closed doors. I think you'd be surprised how non-sexual what we do is."

"Uh-huh, and the moans?" She tilted her head. "That's non-sexual?"

"Can't help it when we bring a woman pleasure without even touching her," Leo said, dripping with so much sexual innuendo I almost rolled my eyes.

"Your loss, baby girl." Finn winked. "Anyway, nothing wrong with making new friends. Let us know if you ever need anything."

Leo walked around her, careful to graze her arm one last time as he and Finn moved past me. Finn whispered under his breath, "She's all ready for you."

Shawn was almost to her door when I approached her; she was doing her best to ignore me and walk fast enough that it didn't look like she was sprinting to get away.

"One minute," I said in a confident voice. "All I need is one minute."

"So you can lecture me on microwave safety again?" She glared.

I liked her spunk.

Almost more than I liked her mocha skin. God, she was beautiful when she was annoyed. That might be my new favorite addiction — annoying her.

"Nah, I think we got that all out of the way last time," I teased before I walked around her body as if I was memorizing her. "Like I said, one minute."

"Fine, but you can't touch me." She smirked.

It was almost unfair how easy it was to read people, even her.

"Agreed." I grinned. "And you don't even have to set the glasses down."

She rolled her eyes. "This I have to see."

"Oh, that's the thing. Your eyes have to be closed. I promise I won't touch you; I'll just give you an idea of what sharing with grownups is like."

She gave me a disgusted look and closed her eyes.

"Fifty-nine seconds," I whispered, holding my hands out in front of me, careful to keep them one inch from her body as I slowly ran them over her arms, her head, her legs. One of the first things I'd learned before signing up for this was Reiki work, or energy-field massages, and from my experience, they worked extremely well on stressed-out college students, especially women.

I moved the energy around her arms, her legs; her body gradually started to slump as her breathing slowed, while I stood behind her and took the negative energy swirling around her head and sent it packing. My fingers heated as I pushed good energy around her face, her lips, her mouth, concentrating on her eyes and the small scar on the right side of her cheek.

Ten seconds.

I moved to the front of her and cupped my hands over

her ears, still without touching her, then ran one hand over her mouth.

Five seconds.

I stood in front of her, my mouth inches from hers.

And I sucked the air between us like the slow burn of a cigarette.

Damn it, she was like nicotine, wasn't she?

"Open," I whispered, still in front of her.

"What…" Her voice croaked as she swayed a bit in front of me. "…the hell was that?"

"You carry a lot of stress in your neck." I touched her then, grabbing the pieces of muscle between my fingers and pressing as she moaned as she sagged forward. "A lot of athletes do. You need to be icing more, all right?"

She nodded against my chest.

Then, as if she'd just realized we were touching, she jerked back and narrowed her gaze. "That's not fighting fair."

"What?" I smirked.

"You." She pointed at me with one of the glasses. "That's like memorizing someone's weakness then pouncing when they're too tired to fight you."

"I have no idea what you're talking about." I wanted to stay. I wanted to fight with her, to argue, to kiss her senseless. Instead, I backed away and nodded my head. "Have a good night, Shawn."

She gaped.

She seemed surprised I wasn't staying.

The struggle was real. After having my hands so close to her body, yet not touching her, my fingers had burned, so I'd broken one of the rules. I'd touched her afterward just to see if her body would respond.

And it had.

Fuck, it had responded beautifully.

She gave her head a shake as her door jerked open.

Slater gave me the same glare I'd been on the receiving end of since the incident freshman year.

I glared right back.

The memories came crashing in, like they always had.

Memories of her smell.

Memories I saw haunting his eyes too.

I looked away.

Backed off.

Because apparently, the universe hated me, and the one girl who'd piqued my interest just happened to be staying with the one guy who had a reason to hate me almost as much as I hated myself.

Wordlessly, he pulled her into the room and slammed the door in my face. I smiled the entire way back to my room and was stunned to find a shocked expression on both my friends' faces.

"You broke a rule." Leo tapped his finger against his chin. "Didn't he, Finn?"

"Yup, sure did."

"I have no idea what you're talking about."

"Bullshit," Finn smirked. "You know you aren't allowed to touch anyone who isn't your client yet, and first-time clients don't get touched after Reiki. They're too vulnerable. So technically, you broke two rules."

"I didn't touch her," I pointed out. "Well, I mean I did but—"

"Ah, and now he's defensive." Finn grinned wider. "Leo, I think I smell a bet coming on."

"Are you twelve?" I spat.

"Fourteen." Leo shrugged. "But he finally got his balls,

so I think we should all celebrate the maturity level in this room."

Finn gave him the finger. "A thousand dollars."

"Make that two." Leo grinned. "Two grand."

"You're both idiots." I looked away. "Besides, I don't need money."

"Then do it because you're bored as fuck and driving us crazy with your mood swings," Finn grumbled.

"What am I even doing?"

"Oh, that's easy. Get her to like you — actually like you — maybe kiss your ugly mug and sleep with you."

I rolled my eyes. "Hell, I could do that half dead."

"No tricks," Leo added. "No Wingman tricks, no Reiki shit, no good touch, no manipulation."

I stared them both down, opened my mouth then closed it again. Because it wasn't something I knew I could actually do by being myself.

The last time I'd actually dated…

Fallen in love.

The last time I had actually been real with a woman…

She'd been taken from me.

They knew it, too.

"No!" I barked as pain filled my chest until it was hard to breathe.

Both of them were quiet as I backed out of the room and slammed the door behind me, feeling like shit and in dire need of a good workout to push the guilt away.

Chapter Seven

Shawn

"Hey there, Shower Girl." Leo sat next to me in Human Anatomy like we were best friends then handed me a coffee. "I asked for Ristretto shots since Knox said you were stressed out. I find the acidic drinks from Starbucks make anxiety higher, thus the sweeter shot."

I blinked. Then blinked harder. He was wearing a tight band shirt, skinny jeans, black and orange combat boots, and a smile that promised more than just moaning, if you get the picture. His golden locks were tucked behind his ears in a low bun, and he was wearing a red beanie that brought out his dark eyebrows and green eyes.

I was more surprised over the fact that women in our general area hadn't suddenly started ripping their shirts off, since just looking at him seemed to send females in to heat.

"Thanks for the coffee." I quickly took it from his hand and looked back at the professor whose name had completely escaped me because the minute Leo sat down, I'd been drenched in the sweetest, most intoxicating cologne I'd ever smelled.

Sweet Lord, what did he do? Sacrifice Channing Tatum on an altar and soak up all his man-juice in a bottle? I clenched my teeth and took a sip of coffee. It was surprisingly sweet with just a hint of sugar that made it easy to swallow.

"Huh?" I pulled it back and stared at Leo. "What was this again?"

"Shower Girl special," he said with a wink. "I'll be more than happy to bring you one every time we have class together." I almost choked. Class together? For the rest of the semester? With him? "But I'm going to need a favor…"

"Is anything ever free?" I wondered out loud.

"You're telling me."

"You're the one asking for a favor."

"How's that coffee? De…li…cious?" He drew out the word, good naturedly teasing me, then leaned in. "So, here's the deal. I need you to seduce Knox."

Had my mouth been full, I would have spit the contents onto the student in front of me and probably soaked my textbook.

"Tell me I heard you wrong," I hissed as the professor started telling everyone what page to open our books to.

Leo shrugged, opened his book before opening mine and founding the correct page. He was… almost too much, but a part of me wondered if he did it out of habit. Was he so used to doing things for women that he just naturally defaulted to gentlemanly actions when his mouth had no choice but to be a jackass?

"Oh you heard me loud and clear, Shower Girl." He gave me some major side-eye then leaned in again. "I'm not saying you have to see what's under his bulging pants."

I felt my face heat.

"Then again, with that reaction, be my fucking guest! Sla-a-ay, woman, slay—"

"Would you keep your voice down!" I pinched him in the side, reverting back to junior high in a seriously embarrassing way.

"I bet you would hold on to his ponytail," he said, completely ignoring me, "like a pony. Hey I can put the song on. You guys can give us a little show—"

I groaned and briefly wondered if I could make a quick escape out the window behind me. "I'm not seducing him."

He opened his mouth and drew a breath.

"Or looking in his pants."

The student in front of me turned around and judged me hardcore; his look of disappointment in the female sex so real that I wanted to punch him in the face.

Leo gave him a stern stare then made a motion with his fingers that said, "*Turn back around ass, or I'm going to let the lady punch you.*"

The guy scowled and turned his back to us.

"College boys," Leo said, as if he wasn't one. "So studious."

"Probably because they want to graduate on time and get a job."

"Oh, I have one of those. Thanks for the advice though." Leo grinned. "Come on, what do you have to lose? All I'm saying is give him a chance. It's been a while…"

"Since he's made a girl moan?" I just had to say.

"Nah." Leo's face turned serious. "Since he's made a girl moan because he wanted to hear it. Since he's been interested enough to approach her rather than the other way around, and in my book, that happened twice in one night because

Little Fort Knox can't keep it locked up forever."

"It?" *Was he talking about the guy's penis?*

Leo reached across the desk and put a hand against my chest. "It." He grinned. "Get your mind out of the gutter."

I sighed. "Say I give him a chance, but no seduction. Do I still get coffee?"

Leo seemed to think about it. "A real chance, not the kind you get just because you're getting coffee every day, along with stellar company."

"Did we establish that you were stellar, though? Can't remember…"

"Cute." He licked his lips. "But I'd like for it to be known that I'm stepping away from the challenge of tasting you, even though I've been dreaming about your tits for at least two nights straight."

"Your bowing out is noted." I rolled my eyes. "And say, 'tits' one more time to me, and I'm going to be twisting one of yours in a very violent non-sexual way, got me?"

"Kinky." He nodded. "I like it. Maybe save that shit for date seven, though. You can't just bust it out on date one. You keep the freak flag inside until it's the right time to let it fly."

"You're just full of great life advice, aren't you?"

He tilted his head. "Aw, that's the nicest thing anyone's ever said to me, and just this morning my mama told me I was smart."

"At least you're pretty." I patted his hand.

He cackled out a laugh, which earned us more stares from classmates and a stern look from the professor.

We were quiet for the next ten minutes.

At least I was quiet.

Leo was too busy tapping his pencil against his book and

sighing like the world was ending because of his boredom.

Class finally dismissed, and I stood.

He crossed his arms, waiting for my answer.

"Fine." I gritted my teeth. "All I can promise is that I'll give him a chance before I knee him in the balls."

"That's really all any man can ask for." He wrapped a warm, bulky arm around me and led me away from other students. The stares I got ranged from jealousy to judgement. I assumed the jealousy was because Leo was touching me, and the judgement was because people no doubt assumed I'd paid for it.

"Skank," one girl whispered.

"Desperate."

I stilled.

Leo turned around so fast you'd have thought he was part cheetah. "You two, over here."

The girls' stunned expressions would have been funny if I hadn't been so embarrassed.

Slowly, they approached us.

"This is Shawn. Say hi, Shawn."

I croaked out a, "Hi," and a weak wave.

"Shawn's my friend. Not my paid cuddle-buddy; not someone I touch because I'm being paid for the fucking honor to touch her, but because I legitimately want to be in her company. So take your bitchy attitudes elsewhere and know that if you ever decide to use our services, we won't answer. You're both blacklisted. I'll be sure to make nice voodoo dolls with your faces on them when I get back to my room, so she can poke your fake boobs with a pin." He grinned wide. "You can go now."

They both scurried off, tears in their eyes, while a few people next to us clapped like it was the best thing they'd seen all day.

He sighed, wrapped an arm around me again, and said, "What's your favorite breakfast food?"

And that was how I became friends with a guy who'd seen me naked before I even knew his name.

Slater was right.

Resistance wasn't an option.

Chapter Eight

Shawn

"FANCY SEEING YOU here of all places," Finn said as he took a seat next to me at the coffee shop. I was trying to study for the test I had almost missed hearing about because stupid Leo wouldn't stop asking me to seduce his friend. Like Knox wasn't a big enough boy to ask himself? Not that he needed to ask.

The whole situation seemed weird.

He could get his own women.

But the way Leo had said it made me wonder if there was more to the story. I just… Ugh! I shouldn't even focus on it; not when I was trying to get an A with a professor who took great joy in giving D's.

I groaned.

These guys were going to be the death of me.

"Huh…" Finn mused. "Not the normal response I get. I mean, there are noises — don't get me wrong — but I don't think they're ever from irritation, unless I just didn't hit the right spot. But to be fair, I like it when girls own their own bodies, you know?"

I was probably gaping at him like a fish. Seriously, what did I ever do to gain their attention other than being the only girl in the suite?

"Studying," I said in a clipped tone. "Don't you have someone else to massage and gain noises from?"

He put a hand over his heart. "I find your concern for my social life both comforting and alarming. Do you want to know who's on the schedule for tonight?"

I shifted in my seat a bit, feeling suddenly hot and cold all at once. Maybe because I wasn't sure how to decipher the attention I was gaining from them, but my body? My body was well on board with whatever they had in mind.

Maybe because I knew that it meant Knox would be a part of whoever the hell was paying them for attention and affection.

"You should come." He leaned in so I was forced to make eye contact. His gaze locked on to mine with an intensity that was almost uncomfortable.

I didn't look away. "Wouldn't that make things weird? Two chicks and three guys? There's going to be a third wheel…"

"Oh, tonight we have two guys."

I literally almost choked on my tongue; in fact, it took me a good five seconds to regain my composure.

"Two," I repeated slowly, trying to sound mature, not ready to blush.

"Yup."

"Guys."

"Naturally."

"What? Because one isn't enough?"

"Damn you're cute. Can I keep you if Knox doesn't have the balls?" He winked. "Seriously come," he pleaded.

"Bet you say that to all the girls," I mumbled.

He burst out laughing. "Careful, your inner wildcat is showing... and according to Leo—"

I slammed my book shut. "Why?"

"I'm confused. What was the question?"

"Why me?" I said slowly. "Is it because I'm an easy target? A transfer who knows nothing about the three of you and your past? Or is it convenience? Slater seems to think you guys like a challenge, but I don't get it. There are loads of beautiful girls on campus. Just pick one and leave me alone."

Please. Because it is getting harder and harder not to fall for all of their little quirks and easy comebacks.

They were beautiful, yes, but not hard to be around; almost like the friends I never knew I'd always wanted, but was now stuck with for the rest of my hellish existence.

"You're like the Bella to our Edward." He smirked.

"I call bullshit," I said in a sweet voice, as I got ready to smack him over the head with the heaviest textbook in my bag. "But nice try."

He laughed, and I couldn't help but join in. Finn's laugh was positively addicting. It lit up the room, and even though it still felt like they were forcing me into a game without telling me all the rules, I genuinely liked his company. Except when I wasn't daydreaming about strangling one, or all, of them.

"Tonight, eight. Be there." He rapped his knuckles on the table and pointed at my book. "Also, just some good advice. Knox aced that class last semester. It's pretty advanced. Leo said you looked stressed. May as well ask the genius out of the three of us for help."

"Are you calling yourself stupid?"

He just grinned. "Honey, I'm heir to a multimillion-dollar fortune and started my own company when I was twelve."

"Twelve?"

"I was one of the original YouTube toy players, made bank on those videos — even picked my nose in one when I didn't know Mom was filming." He winked. "Don't be late, Shower Girl. I'd hate for you to miss out on the festivities."

"Is that what the kids are calling it these days?"

He didn't answer. Just bent down and brushed a kiss across my cheek as if it was the most normal thing in the world, then whispered in my ear, "Your skin drives him mad, you know."

"Who?" I asked breathlessly.

"Knox." He pulled back until I was lost in his gaze again. "You're chocolate milk, and baby girl, he's been thirsting for a long time."

With that, he left, and once again, my mouth was unattractively hanging open, all the things I'd just read completely forgotten.

Chapter Nine

Knox

"What the hell do you mean you invited her?" I put on my typical uniform — tight ripped jeans, a white T-shirt that left nothing to the imagination — and pulled my hair back into a man bun that made me want to die a little bit each time I did it.

I liked short hair.

But, per Wingman, Inc. rules, I needed to be the rockstar of the three, the grumpy un-obtainable one who made the clients come back wanting, thinking just one more visit would win the biggest treasure among the three of us.

Fuck my life. I hated being the damn treasure almost as much as I hated this internship.

One. More. Semester.

Finn shrugged. "She was stressed out over Human Anatomy. Thought this might perk her up."

Yeah, in more ways than one.

Five guys in a small dorm room without AC. What could go wrong?

I coughed when Leo sprayed the room with lavender while Finn lit two candles and started stretching like we were getting ready for the annual Track and Field Open.

One. More. Semester.

A soft knock sounded at the door.

I pasted a surly look on my face then jerked open the door as our two clients stood outside wringing their hands, apparently confused as to what to do with them. They were attractive enough, freshman dudes who really needed to learn the hard way how to stop getting dumped.

It wasn't that they desired our attention sexually.

They just wanted to learn how to be like us.

So, we gave them lessons.

And we showed them how to touch, how to listen, how to look — the Holy Grail of dating lessons. It helped that we were trying to groom at least one of them to take my spot next year. They both had the looks — striking features, tall, muscular — but they were seriously lacking in the confidence department. I wanted this lesson over so I could finish with our next client and take a long sleep.

"Chris, Jay, come on in." I opened the door wide and nearly slammed it shut before I noticed Shawn standing right behind them, arms crossed, judgement so evident on her face it made me crack a smile. Just what the hell did she think we did behind closed doors?

"You coming?" I leaned against the doorframe and crossed my arms. *Please say no, please say no.* I wouldn't be able to concentrate worth shit.

"I was pondering it…" Her eyes narrowed. "…mainly because I have a proposition for you after, and I'm curious if I want to get involved with someone who…" She didn't explain.

"Proposition." My eyebrows shot up. "Color me intrigued."

"Yeah, well…" Her cheeks went red as she looked down at her shoes and finally back up at me. "Human Anatomy is killing me, no exaggeration. You're going to find my body one of these days under the textbook just suffocating."

I smirked.

"Laugh all you want, but I need— I would pay you— I mean—"

"Prove to me you can hang around this…" I pointed behind me. "…and I'll do it for free." I'd almost said, *"I'd do you for free."*

Damn it, Knox, rein it in!

"Really?" She perked up as if I'd just offered sex on a silver platter, with free orgasms.

"Really." I found myself smiling.

I rarely smiled.

I wanted to hate her for it.

I cleared my throat and opened the door wider.

She peeked under my arm then gave me a wary look.

"Aw, come on. Your innocence is showing." I winked. "Just promise you won't repeat what you see here."

Her eyes went so round I had to look away to keep myself from laughing out loud.

Finally, she gulped and stepped into the room.

Finn had one of our desk chairs pulled out for her, indicating he'd known she would come, and Leo just winked at me like he was solving world hunger by inviting a girl into our room.

I rolled my eyes and turned to Chris and Jay, who literally

could not take their eyes off Shawn, even if they'd wanted to.

Yeah, I understood that feeling all too well.

She had gorgeous wavy black-and-brown hair, what could only be called voluptuous lips, and innocent-looking eyes that slammed into me so hard it was almost freaky. And her body? Don't even get me started on those legs, those breasts. She was the perfect package of hot chocolate with marshmallows, and I was freezing my ass off for a taste.

"So…" I rubbed my hands together. "…Jay, how did this week go?"

I shot a glance to Shawn, who looked so confused it was almost cute.

"Well…" His eyes flickered away from Shawn as indecision warred across his face. "I just… I think I come on too strong. I was with a chick—"

"Woman," Finn corrected. "They're never chicks, you insensitive prick. Try again."

"Woman." He cleared his throat. "Classy woman." His eyes were wide. Damn, I needed to dirty him up if he was going to join the team when I graduated. "Things were going great. We were laughing, joking around… then I reached for her hand, and she flinched."

Leo grinned. "Show me how much of a flinch." He held out his hand.

Jay took it hesitantly then jolted back.

"Fear," Finn sighed. "You surprised her, man. Sounds like you were coming in hot with the jokes." He sighed. "Joke, joke, joke, sex." He shook his head. "Not how women work, my friend."

"But—" The jackass actually looked confused. "—I thought you guys said humor's the easiest way to break boundaries?"

"Emotional boundaries," I jumped in. "Not physical."

"Oh." Jay nodded. "So next time I warn her?"

Groaning, Leo covered his face with his hands. Then he dropped his hands and marched over to Shawn, keeping his eyes on Jay. "Watch and take notes."

He was about an inch from Shawn's chair. Her breathing grew heavy as he leaned down and said, "Pretend I'm joking with you, Shower Girl. We're having a good time. I'm sending you signals. What's the only thing I'm going to be able to do that won't freak you out, or seem too fast?"

She chewed her lower lip. The sight of those even white teeth with the almost invisible gap in front gave me ideas of—

Shit, concentrate!

Then a gleam of speculation entered her eyes, showing she was actually thinking about it. Helping. "Off the top of my head?"

"Yup." Leo's eyes twinkled, damn him.

She groaned, and my jeans began to strangle me in a sweet, slow death. "Soft brush of your hand," she mumbled.

Leo was smiling so hard I wanted to pummel him. "So, like this?" He ran his knuckles down the side of her arm then pulled away.

Her breath hitched as she nodded. A visible tremor rippled down her body, and I gritted my teeth against the one that threatened to run through me. Palms sweating, I focused in on her breathing, the soft part of her lips as she physically responded, obviously without even thinking about it.

Fuck. The things I could do to her.

Jay's eyes narrowed, and his tongue touched his upper lip. I could almost hear him asking to test the move himself as he leaned in, waiting, his eyes dilated with lust. "And then what?"

"Walk away," I said curtly. "You walk away, let them wonder if it was accidental—"

"Or on purpose," Shawn finished, surprising me.

A hint of admiration took the sexual edge off, and I nodded as Finn jumped next to Leo, flanking Shawn's other side.

"The only other way to make the hand holding work is by making something up." He teased Shawn's other arm with his knuckles then grabbed her hand and said, "Wow, your fingers are so delicate. You must play the piano? Right?"

Shawn smiled.

Holy shit, does she really play the piano?

How had I missed that?

I stared down at her fingers.

They were long, thin, delicate.

"Good guess," she breathed out the words as Finn continued to link their fingers together and moved in.

His lips met the side of her cheek then grazed downward as he continued talking. "Now, Jay, this is another pivotal moment. You want her to feel pleasure, but remember our number one rule. We don't go beyond the walls of the skin, right? So, you let…" He nuzzled her neck, drawing in a long, slow breath as his nose toyed with her skin.

She froze and locked eyes with me.

I wondered if she imagined my mouth, my lips.

Hell, I'm imagining that scenario.

Then her lips parted. But she wasn't pressing in to him; she was leaning toward me.

I smiled. *Ah, sweet victory.* She hadn't jerked away because she was under Finn's spell, but because she was under mine.

Mine.

Mine.

Mine.

So even though I was ready to break a desk over Finn's head, I let him instruct our new guys.

"You let them feel every sensation through your touch, and I guarantee it will be enough for them to ask for more. We don't screw our clients. We just show them how it's supposed to be when they're with their match, and hopefully, after a few sessions, they sign up for the Wingman, Inc. app. You get kickbacks for each client who signs up for the dating service, and you also have a killer job recommendation." He pulled back.

Shawn gulped and adjusted in her chair then folded her hands in her lap and shot me a murderous glare. I love that she hated her treacherous body almost as much as I loved that she still couldn't take her eyes off me.

"All right." I cleared my throat and pointed to Chris. "You're up. How'd it go?"

He exhaled slowly. "I did everything in the manual you guys gave me. It was going so well. In fact, I was pretty sure she was almost too into me when things went south."

"South?" I repeated in shock. "Things should never, and I mean *never*, go south…"

"No." Chris actually blushed and ran a hand through his blond locks. "I mean they went south as in she yelled at me, tried to punch me, and ran off."

"You were reading her all wrong then." I shrugged. "If things are going well, they don't just sour. You sure she wasn't playing you?"

He frowned. "We've sat next to each other for the last semester, eaten together, gone on multiple coffee dates. I've kissed her on the cheek—"

"Yeah…" Leo grinned widely. "…I'm going to stop you right there. Friend Zone."

Chris groaned into his hands.

"A kiss on the cheek is harmless. Hell, it's European." Leo spread his arms wide. "She thought you were a safe place, and you ruined it by asking for more. You need to learn how to read the signs better. Watch and learn." He walked up to Shawn and tried to pull her in for a kiss. She smacked him away then stood and stomped on his foot.

I choked on my laugh while Leo hopped on one foot and said, "See? Totally not ready for a kiss."

"Count me out!" Finn held his hands up in surrender.

I didn't need to push the point any further, but the way that Shawn looked at me, with challenge in the chocolatey depths of her eyes… well, I couldn't really back down.

Instead, I sauntered over to her, leaned closer, and kissed the top of her head.

She went completely still as I whispered, "If the girl leans into you and doesn't even realize she's doing it…" Shawn was doing exactly that. "…feel free to slowly build your case with her. It means she's into it. But if she jerks away, or if she seems confused why you'd hit on her, you need to go back into the safe zone and try again later. These women are ones we want to feel safe around you, so that when they break up with their boyfriends — and they will, especially freshmen — they come running to you for comfort of every variety except sexual then you help them decide which direction to take in their next relationship."

"And that direction," Finn said, "will always be Wingman, Inc., unless they aren't interested in a relationship. Then your job is to be a support for them until they are." He offered a matter-of-fact shrug. "Some may never get there. You may have clients who literally only rely on you to get by each week — but that's the job."

Finn coughed into his hand, and I became aware that I was running my hand along Shawn's bare shoulder.

I jerked away then tugged her hair a bit.

Her breath hitched.

She liked it.

I loved it.

"So…" Leo rubbed his hands together. "…that's enough tutoring for tonight. Keep us updated, all right?"

Chris and Jay both stood and walked out of the room.

Leaving the three of us alone with Shawn.

And her sitting there like a lamb at slaughter.

Chapter Ten

Shawn

I sat back down, dumbfounded.

So when guys came in? They just trained them on how to get women? Or how to send them to that crazy dating app? It seemed like a scam, but at the same time, they created this sense of trust and safety that had everyone eating out of their hands. People still left satisfied, and that was all that mattered? It made sense, I guessed, in a way, but I wasn't sure how that built Knox's case. I mean, he helped other guys get the girl, but it seemed dishonest. Didn't it?

I frowned harder when another knock sounded at the door. No one bothered answering, and a gorgeous woman with slick, black hair and crystal blue eyes bounced in.

"My favorite girl!" Leo tugged her into his arms and kissed her on the mouth as if it was normal. Finn followed, twirling her into the air as Knox moved away from me in their direction.

My chest constricted as I waited for him to politely push her away. Instead, he pulled her into his arms and pressed his mouth, hot and eager, against hers.

And just like that…

I was done.

Game over.

The end.

Now I understood the warnings Slater had given me.

The reason he wanted me far, far, away.

Because *this* to them was normal, and I wasn't into sharing, no matter how seductive it might look. They'd made me feel — special.

And it suddenly occurred to me. That was just what they did.

And they freaking got paid for it!

Disgusted, I stood and shoved past everyone, ready to slam the door behind me, when Knox suddenly grabbed my elbow and jerked me around. "What?" he sneered. "Can't handle it?"

"Handle what?" I tried to sound unaffected. "I'm just not in to that scene. Good for you, though, working your way through college. I hope it all turns out for you."

"So that's it?" His grin looked more pissed than friendly. "You're just… done? No tutoring? No friendship with Finn and Leo?"

"I think…" I looked behind him as both Leo and Finn stood on either side of the beautiful girl; one kissed her neck while the other grabbed her hands. "…that you guys have enough friends."

I hated that my chest was tight.

Almost as much as I hated that I had tears in the backs of my eyes for no stupid reason. These guys weren't mine.

But for two straight days, I'd fallen for it.

Fallen for the attention they gave everyone. The only difference? They'd given it to me for free.

"So. Stupid!" I roared the minute I got back to my room, seconds after slamming my door.

"Told you so," Slater said from the bed, textbook open, beanie almost completely over his eyes, and coffee in his right hand. "They're the devil, all of them."

"How the hell can they get away with that?" I grabbed his unicorn and whacked it against the wall.

"Hey now, don't take it out on Horny."

I dropped the unicorn onto the floor. "You named your unicorn Horny?"

"It has a horn." He shrugged. "Besides, aren't all animals horny?"

"Are you asking?"

He yawned. "And to answer your question, they get away with this little business because Wingman, Inc. gives the school millions of dollars a year in order to have a presence on campus. Get this, in the last three years alone, they've tripled their enrollment for the dating app. Who cares if the success rate is high? They're manipulating people into using it."

"But the people who use it are happy?" I wondered aloud.

"Does it matter? Manipulation is manipulation."

I suddenly felt sick to my stomach.

Slater must have noticed because he got off his bed, put his cup down on the nightstand then braced my shoulders with both hands. "I'm sorry. I don't know what else to say except I warned you."

"And I still fell for it," I grumbled. "How stupid do you think I am? On a scale of one to ten?"

"Solid middle ground." His lips twitched. "To be fair, they're pretty to look at, and sometimes raccoons just can't help themselves when they see the shiny."

"Hey—" I playfully shoved him away. "—are you calling me a raccoon?"

He grinned. "Little bit, yeah."

"Fair." I groaned and pulled him back in for a hug. He smelled like spicy soap and Starbucks coffee.

When he released me, it was with a small smile on his face. "Tell you what. Let's order pizza tonight. You can wallow in the greasy goodness."

"With extra cheese?" I countered.

"And pineapple." He groaned like he was going to have an orgasm from the mere thought of pineapple on extra cheese pizza.

"Weirdo." I punched him on the arm and thought back to the training session. Slater was good-looking. Not just handsome; some might even say hot. "Why didn't you get asked to work with them?"

When he didn't answer, I turned around.

Slater's stance was completely frozen as he held the unicorn with one hand and his cell in the other.

"Slater?"

He gave his head a shake and offered me a forced smile. "Would you believe me if I told you I didn't always hate them?"

"No." I burst out laughing. "Is it true?"

He just shrugged and said quietly, "I don't even know anymore…"

That was the last conversation we had about it before we ate pizza while talking about school, unicorns, and him helping me find a tutor.

But when we turned the lights out, I wondered.

I wondered why he looked so sad.

And why he always seemed so pissed in the guys' presence; maybe they'd done something to personally offend him other than just exist in the same space.

I opened my mouth to pry more, when I heard his soft snores.

Tomorrow. I'd ask again tomorrow.

Chapter Eleven

Knox

"WHAT THE HELL were you thinking?" Leo sent a pillow sailing toward my face later that night when I was trying to get ready for bed.

I dodged it just in time for it to hit Finn, who collapsed to the floor in a heap of middle fingers.

I jumped into bed with my phone. "No idea what you're talking about."

"The hell you do," Finn said from the floor. "You never kiss the girls, ever. It's one of your rules, and you kissed Jessica! You hate Jessica, say it on a daily basis. She's been after your ass for years, and you kissed her. Why?"

I knew why.

They probably did too.

It had been a dick move. Instinctual. Because I'd felt vulnerable. Because I'd wanted *her* to think the worst of me. Because I couldn't stand being in the same small room with her without touching her, without wanting her, and I couldn't go down that path again.

Especially after the last one had ended so horribly.

So, I'd defaulted to the asshole I was — and kissed a girl I'd had no intention of ever touching again, a girl who I knew would reciprocate and shock the hell out of Shawn.

I had purposefully hurt her.

I knew it.

What I hadn't expected?

Was for it to hurt me as much as it had.

Shawn was a stranger to me, and yet I saw the pain in her eyes, felt it slam into me in waves as I stood there and waited for her to rage, to yell, to do something, maybe to save me from myself.

But she'd walked away.

Proving yet another point.

They either die.

Or walk away.

Nobody stayed.

Nobody.

"Forget about it." I set my alarm and shrugged them off. "I was just trying to gauge where Jessica was at, and she's not in this for a relationship. She wants all of us, and she's past the year mark." Hell, technically she was way past it. "I say we have the talk with her. She can keep using our services for a higher rate with no touching, only talk therapy, or she can sign up for Wingman, Inc. I'll talk her through all the positives, and we'll see what happens."

"That's a bunch of bullshit." Leo yawned. "I'll let you have it, though."

"We both will," Finn said in a tortured voice as if he knew the reasons why, which meant I needed to hide my emotions even more than I already had.

"Night, guys."

"Night, Knox," they said after one another.

When I closed my eyes, I could see the pain on Shawn's face, and watched as that face transformed into the familiar nightmare of the last three years.

And once again, I slept like shit.

Because I spent the entire night trying to save someone who was already dead.

Always too late.

Always.

Chapter Twelve

Shawn

IT WAS HAPPENING again.

The moaning.

I put a pillow over my face and screamed.

Not because it was too loud.

But because I kept wondering who was causing it. One? Two? All three? Leo and Finn had both tried to talk to me in class and at the coffee shop again. I'd brushed them off but been polite.

And Knox?

Well, let's just say that Knox had suddenly turned over a leaf that said, *"Go out of my way to make Shawn's life miserable."*

He was suddenly everywhere.

And with a different female every single day.

It drove me insane.

Bat-shit crazy.

And he wasn't even mine to go senseless over!

The moan happened again.

"That's it!" I got up from my bed, stomped over to the door, and jerked it open. Then I stormed my way over to their room and almost took down the door with my pounding.

When Leo answered, he grinned down at me. "Come to play?"

I gave him the finger.

His eyes narrowed. "I'm confused. Is that yes or no?"

"Agh!" I threw my hands up in the air. "I have practice tomorrow at five in the morning It's three. I've had one hour of sleep. Can you *please* keep the moaning to a minimum?"

"You seem stressed." He tilted his head just as Finn joined him in the doorway. "Doesn't she?"

"Very." Finn nodded then reached out and started massaging my right shoulder muscle while Leo grabbed my hand and worked my fingers. It felt so damn good that I forgot I was pissed for about two seconds before I pulled away.

"No." I jabbed my finger at each of their chests. "Shame on you. Stop using your skills to make me less crazy. I need sleep."

"I could not agree more." Leo put his hand over his chest. "If you want, I can come over and—"

"No!" I made a fist with my hands. "I don't need you to help me sleep. I need you to keep your clients quiet so that I *can* sleep. Big difference."

Knox appeared then and held out a pair of Bose noise-canceling headphones. "You can borrow them every Friday as long as you don't set them on fire when you're done."

"Do you think I really want whatever STDs are crawling around the surface?" I hissed.

His eyes turned lethal. "Then I guess you won't sleep."

"Dun, dun, dun," Finn sang in a low voice, just as a small lady who could pass as my grandmother made an appearance and shoved a fifty-dollar bill in Knox's pants then patted him on his rock-hard six-pack. She had a full-on red wig perched backward on her head and cherry red cheeks with black glasses that she kept shoving up her nose. And her purse looked like something I would have seen on *I Love Lucy*. It was this giant black clutch that probably held cough drops and prunes.

"Thanks, boys."

"Love you, Edna!" Finn called while Leo brushed a kiss across her hand.

She finger-waved at Knox and straight-up waddled out of the suite.

I stared after her, my jaw dropping with each step she took until she was out of eyesight.

"What…" I shook my head. "…I mean, seriously, guys, what?"

Finn's eyes got serious. "She's lonely."

"She's at least eighty!" I yelled, so exhausted I was actually arguing with crazy.

Knox got all up in my business and said through clenched teeth, "Her husband died a year ago. She's not comfortable with internet dating yet. We're easing her in because she wants a partner for life, someone she can laugh with, so if we can give her that one laugh, that nice touch once a week, we're going to fucking do it. Now jump off that pedestal, take the damn Bose, and go to sleep."

He slammed the headphones in my hand and followed with the door, leaving me staring at a swinging white board with a black marker and a giant heart on it with their names scribbled in fan-girl cursive.

I glared at their names a good two minutes before I turned on my heel and went back to bed.

And I hated myself a little bit more when I lifted the headphones to my face and smelled Knox on them, made the mistake of inhaling again then stupidly sat them on my desk, which just so happened to be next to my pillow, and my head.

I slept soundly for the first time in days.

Chapter Thirteen

Knox

I FELT LIKE shit and wanted someone to blame other than the bastard staring back at me in the mirror. Jessica wouldn't let it rest and threatened to sue. So, all in all? I wasn't having the best Tuesday of my life.

It had been a little less than a week since the huge fight with Shawn.

She still had my headphones.

And a sick part of me liked that she had something of mine, even if it was to make sure she didn't have to hear what I did for a living. I groaned and made my way into class.

I was the TA for Professor Duke, and yes, that was his real name. Grumpy old bastard got a nice thrill out of flunking people.

"Knox?" He crooked his finger at me.

"Yeah?"

He didn't say anything else, just handed me a stack of

papers and an answer key then looked back at his computer.

"Right." I rolled my eyes and made my way over to one of the free desks and started the tedious work of grading papers.

I was about two hours in when I saw her name.

Shawn.

It was scribbled in pretty handwriting that matched her skin and lips. Handwriting I traced with my finger a dozen times before I got to work.

The first three answers were wrong.

I winced as I kept grading, and when I tallied up her score, I felt so bad for her I wanted to accidentally lose the test so she could do a retake.

Sixty-eight percent.

Not exactly the best grade on the planet, though she still did better than most people in the class who got lower than a fifty percent.

I finished up the grading then entered the percentages into the online Blackboard site and called it a day, just as Professor Duke was leaving.

"Hey, Duke." I was one of the rare ones he let call him by name.

"Knox?" He turned and rubbed his tired eyes with his free hand then returned his glasses. "Finished already?"

"Yeah." I crossed my arms over my bulky chest. "I actually was just wondering if you needed me to help tutor anyone? This test was rough for a lot of students."

Total bullshit. What I really wanted to ask was if he could please force me to tutor a certain girl so she had no choice but to say yes.

He sighed. "That bad, huh?"

I snorted. "What did you expect? The test was seven pages long."

He grinned. "I like testing their mental fortitude."

"Achieved." I laughed. "Trust me, there will be tears."

"Bah!" He waved a hand at me. "The world is full of tears. This is where we mold students to fight past them, am I right?"

He gave me a knowing glance.

I looked away and mumbled, "Right."

"There are a few who have asked. I'll email you some names tonight, and you can see if your schedule meshes with any of them."

"Great." I tried not to look too eager.

I must have failed because his eyes narrowed. "And you're just doing this out of the goodness of your heart?"

I winked. "You wound me."

"Uh-huh." He sputtered out a laugh. "Day's over, Knox. Get out of my hair."

The man was bald.

I left with a wave anyway.

And whistled all the way to my Mercedes coupe.

Chapter Fourteen

Shawn

I TAPPED MY pencil against my thigh as I waited in the library for my tutor to show. His or her email was DukeTA@wsu.edu, so I had no clue if I was getting a male or female, and honestly? I didn't care. I'd bombed my last test and between practices, weightlifting sessions, and the crazies across the suite, I was slowly losing my mind.

When did college students even have time to do all the things? Especially college athletes?

I grunted, cracking my neck so that some of the tension would release from my shoulders and all the tight muscles. I flipped open my textbook then checked my phone again.

Two minutes to five.

I huffed out a breath when I checked my cell again and saw it had been another five minutes. Still a no-show. And then, as if I had conjured up the devil himself, I looked up into Knox's hypnotic blue eyes and gaped. "Can I help you?"

He set down the same, exact textbook I had and slid an iced coffee toward me. "I think that's my line."

I grabbed the coffee, clenched it actually, almost afraid it was poison, or worse, some sort of drug that would make me hump his leg. *Yeah, that would be just awesome.* "Pardon?"

"Can I help you?" he said slowly, leaning in and licking his lips. "Now, if you open to Chapter Three—"

"Wait, wait!" I looked around the busy library as if it was some sick joke, and someone was going to pop out and say, *"Gotcha!"* "I told you I didn't need you."

"And you nearly failed your last test. Trust me, I graded it." He shrugged, apparently trying to disregard the fact that it was extremely embarrassing that he'd gone over all of my crap answers and marked them with an angry red pen. "Professor Duke paired me with students who need help. Thus, here I am."

I deflated.

So, he was here doing his job as the TA? I mean, of course he was. Why did it matter? I was just another job. *Fantastic.* This would be a good thing. I shifted in my seat. A great thing, even. I cleared my throat and said, "You could have told me you were the TA."

"A guy has to have his secrets." He smirked then sipped his own iced coffee and grabbed a notebook from his messenger bag. His blond hair kept falling out of his messy man bun. It was a seriously strong temptation to use my fingers to brush that hair back. "Like I said, Chapter Three…"

"R-right." I cleared my throat and turned to the correct page then waited as he started firing off definitions and study techniques for Duke's test.

He was talking so fast that I had to put a hand up. "Wait, say that again." I wrote down as much as I could and tried not to be intimidated by his obvious intelligence compared to my own stupidity when it came to the material.

Two hours later, he was yawning, and my neck felt like someone had sat on it then twisted for good measure. I dug my left hand into the muscles while my right kept taking the last of the notes he had for me.

When I looked up, he was gone.

And then massive warm hands were on my back.

And I was so sore I didn't even jerk away; instead, I moaned out, "This in the TA job description?"

"It is now," he said gruffly, moving his massive hands along my tight muscles as if he was studying how to be a massage therapist and not... Wait. What was his major? I frowned.

"What's your major?"

"Business Marketing and Management with a double minor in Human Anatomy and Psychology.

I groaned. "Show off."

His laugh was deep, rich. It felt real, a comforting blanket you wrap around yourself on a cold fall day. "Yeah well, I like to understand how both the mind and body work, and I know business is just a smart major to have."

I nodded. "That's... great."

His hands moved slower this time. I looked around the library. The lights were lower than before, the sun gone, and only a handful of students scattered about. I had finally relaxed a little when the rain started pouring outside.

Ugh! I'll have to walk in that.

Thunder sounded.

And just like that...

The electricity flickered and went off.

I gripped the table with my hands while Knox stopped

massaging and trailed his hand down my arm then faced me. "Hey, you okay?"

"Uh, yes," I said in a shaky voice. "I'm just not a huge fan of the dark."

"And here you seem so fearless to me," he whispered, closer than before. I could almost feel his lips on mine.

What was happening?

I could barely see the outline of his face.

He traced a finger down my jaw and whispered, "Good job today."

"Thanks."

Talk about crossing a line.

"We can meet a few times a week to keep you fresh, all right?"

Wait, was he leaving me?

I quickly grabbed him by the forearm.

He covered my hand with his. "What's wrong?"

"Oh!" Suddenly embarrassed, I tried to pull back. "I, um, thought you were leaving me."

"Is that really how you see me? The guy who abandons innocent girls in the dark?"

"What makes you think I'm innocent?" I fired back stupidly.

He ran a knuckle down the side of my cheek then very casually drifted lower to my chest near my breast.

I shivered.

"That. Right there."

"Maybe I'm cold."

"Or innocent."

I gritted my teeth. "Let's just go with cold and a bit terrified of dark shapes attacking me and dragging me into the creepy basement."

"Not so creepy when you're down there making out," he said with a chuckle.

I shivered and wrapped my arms around my middle. "How long do you think the lights will be out?"

"Who knows?" I could feel him standing next to me then the flashlight of his cell was on as he packed both of us up and held out his hand. "Let's go."

"Go?" I repeated slowly. "Go where?"

"Back to the dorm. I'll drive."

"That's okay. I can—"

"Shawn, you live in the exact, same suite as me. Do you really think I'm that much of a jackass that I'd watch you walk in the cold rain while I speed past you?"

I didn't answer. Because I wasn't sure what type of guy he was. I still couldn't figure it out. He was both tender and aggressive, dangerous and deep. I was completely out of my element, and it was starting to mess with my logic.

Because logically speaking, he was bad news.

But did a guy who was bad news tutor someone out of the goodness of his heart?

"Okay." I put on my hoodie, grabbed my bag, and followed him out of the library.

He ran ahead of me. Lights flickered from a beautiful silver Mercedes coupe that probably cost more than my entire college education.

Of course he couldn't be normal and just own a bike.

Or an old Toyota.

No, he had to have a Mercedes.

Naturally.

He opened the door for me.

I slid across light brown leather and tried not to be the crazy person who feels all the soft edges just to see if the stitching's hand sewn.

He got in, turned on my seat warmer, and the engine roared to life.

The car even felt expensive.

It smelled like him.

My posture was stiff as he peeled out of the parking lot and made a turn in the opposite direction of our dorm.

"Um…" I pointed. "…weren't you supposed to take a left?"

"Yes, backseat driver, I was. But I'm starving."

"And now I'm your prisoner?"

He just grinned and said, "I'll give you fries."

My stomach chose that exact moment to growl with determination, since I clearly wasn't speaking up about my favorite food group.

"Athletes need to carb up. Think of it as a way to take your mind off the dark, stormy night and keep it on more important things."

"Like high-calorie foods with ketchup?"

"Like…" He licked his lips and pulled into Wendy's. "…maybe not hating your suite-mates as much as you could or should."

"Ha." I suppressed a laugh. "Easier said than done since my suite-mates like to kiss anything with a pulse."

"Hey, I'll have you know Edna tips very well."

"I bet." I shuddered. "Does she take out her dentures beforehand, or do you like them in better?"

He made a gagging noise. "Edna likes to talk. She keeps them in. We massage her a bit, tell her how wonderful she is — all true by the way — and she leaves completely satisfied."

"Huh." I couldn't argue that; the woman had looked one second away from floating out of the room on an orgasm-fueled cloud. Gross.

"Want anything other than fries?" Knox looked over at me.

I got lost in those stupid blue eyes again, and that man bun that made him look like he was getting ready to try out for the next Marvel movie. He definitely had the muscle tone to give Chris Hemsworth a run for his money.

"Um…"

He just smiled, ignored me, and ordered me a cheeseburger, fries, and a Coke. Not diet. I almost kissed him right then and there.

"I can pay for—"

His hand shot out so fast I dropped my bag back by my feet.

"No. You never pay. Not for anything. Not with me, not with Leo, not with Finn, and if I ever hear you do, I'll hand them their asses, all right? Those pieces of shit should know better anyway."

Okay, so now it was personal? Women paying for stuff?

"I invited you here. I drove here. That means your money's no good." He shrugged, handed over a black credit card then grabbed the food and receipt.

The entire car filled with the smell of fast food. I inhaled greedily. I'd been trying to be really good lately with eating on campus, so basically fries smelled like crack to me right about now.

Knox drove us back to the dorms and pulled into a parking spot just as Slater parked his bike in a spot across from us.

It was one of those Suzuki bikes people race on.

Who knew the guy could ride?

He pulled off his helmet, leaving his caramel hair sticking

out all over as he witnessed me getting out of Knox's car and Knox carrying food.

"He's my tutor," I blurted like a child caught red-handed in some forbidden activity.

Knox's lips twitched, while Slater looked less than pleased.

"Yeah?" Slater crossed his arms. "What kind?"

"The kind with books, dumbass." Knox rolled his eyes. "Get your head out of your ass."

Slater's eyes narrowed at Knox, as he fell into step beside me. When we all got on the elevator, he stood between us like a chaperone, as though I needed protection from Knox.

The three of us walked into the suite to the sound of Leo and Finns loud laughter. , They were watching something in the communal living room on the flat screen I gulped as Leo muted the TV.

The entire room fell silent.

But electric.

Awkward was an understatement.

"Hey, man." Finn, for the first time since I'd met him, looked sad. And Leo? Well, he looked like someone had just run over his puppy as he nodded to Slater as if he was guilty of something. But it wasn't as bad as Knox's face.

Which held complete devastation when Slater gave us his back, stomped straight into our room, and slammed the door.

I was still staring after him as Knox handed me my food and pointed toward my room. "You should get some sleep."

He was excusing me.

Sending me away.

What did I expect though?

We weren't anything.

Never would be.

"Thanks for the food." I didn't give them a backward glance as I followed Slater, but I did hear one of the guys groan, and I could have sworn someone got punched.

It made me smile.

Only until I saw Slater's pale face.

And noticed his shaking hands.

"What's wrong?" I dropped the food on the table and hesitantly walked over to him.

He squeezed the unicorn then tossed it across the room like it was offensive.

"Everything," he whispered hoarsely. "And the fact that history has no choice but to repeat itself, right?" He didn't look me in the eye, just laid down on his bed with all his clothes on and said, "Remember that I warned you, Shawn. This time, I did my part. This time, I'm not guilty."

We didn't speak for the rest of the night.

Chapter Fifteen

Knox

EVERY TIME I saw his face, I saw hers.

It was unfortunate.

I often wondered what he thought when he saw my face. Did he see the friendship that used to exist in the empty unspoken space between us? Or just death?

My fries tasted like sand in my mouth.

The burger, I ended up tossing to Finn, who couldn't even stomach it enough to take one bite.

We were all quiet.

The three of us.

And for the first time in years, we had a free night.

Which meant we had nothing but our thoughts and fuck-ups to keep us company.

"Do you think he'll ever get over it?" Finn asked, throwing a basketball in the air every few seconds and catching it, only to throw it again.

Leo shifted in his chair; it creaked under his weight as he looked to me then back at the cheap tan carpet. "If we're not over it, he sure as shit isn't over it."

I sighed. "We should go to a party or something."

Both guys looked at me as if I'd just grown a third nipple.

"Knox Tate?" Leo said with a gasp. "Party? You don't party. You sulk. Sure you don't have a fever?"

"Very funny." I rolled my eyes. "I don't know, we have a free night tonight. It just seems—"

"Better than sitting here thinking thoughts," Finn finished for me.

We all stared at each other then jumped to our feet and grabbed all of our shit. Sometimes memories were the worst company you could have, especially when paired with mistakes you couldn't take back.

I was the last to leave the room. I'd taken two steps toward her door when Finn pulled me back.

"Maybe it's for the best. Maybe there's a reason she's his roommate…"

"Yeah," I croaked, "maybe."

"I miss it too," Finn said in a low voice. "We all do."

"Right." Anger punched me in the gut first, followed by regret as I slammed the door behind me and looked straight ahead. I either needed to get drunk, or laid, or both.

And what better place to do that than Greek Row?

We were there in minutes.

Our choice of party.

"Four parties, three look ready to be shut down already, which is a bit early if you ask me." Leo shrugged. "But…" He pointed to our old frat from freshman year. "…at least we know they don't put shit in their beer."

"Cheers to that." We bumped fists then the three of us

walked up to the house and in the front door.

It was one thing I would never get tired of.

The sheer power behind what we did.

The way that the other guys obviously wished they were us every pathetic day of their lives, and the way the woman sucked their lips the minute they saw us smile in their direction.

If royalty existed on campus...

We were it.

To the guys, we were gods; to the women, unobtainable. It worked well in our favor and worked really well for Wingman, Inc.

"YES!" Eli, the house president, shouted over the music. "Our prodigals are home!"

Cheers surrounded us as we moved through the crowd. Girls tried to grab; guys glared at their girlfriends for fanning themselves. All in all, it was turning out to be a great night.

I made my way toward the keg and grabbed a cup.

Leo and Finn followed, though they looked like they'd both just been groped; Leo's button-down shirt was legit missing its top three buttons, and the top button of Finn's jeans was undone.

"I forget how crazy girls get." Leo wiped some lipstick from his neck. "It's like a free-for-all buffet whenever we go out."

"For them," Finn added as he buttoned his jeans back together.

I eyed the room over the rim of my cup and surveyed all the dancing bodies ripe with sweat, right along with the smell of alcohol, Axe Body Spray, bad choices, and fake tans. My mind buzzed from the taste of the alcohol.

I shouldn't have taken a sip.

Because taste, smell… they always brought me back.

Back to the beginning.

Back to the end.

"What's your name?" I handed the beautiful girl a drink. She had autumn-colored hair and an easy, wide smile that was impossible not to return.

"Ah, I don't share such private information." She winked, took a sip, scrunched up her nose, and leaned in. "Got anything better?"

"In my room," I tried.

She burst out laughing. "That work on all the drunk freshman girls?"

"It would sure as hell work on a drunk freshman guy." I pointed at myself then held out my hand. "Knox Tate, and you are?"

"Sophie." She chewed her lower lip. "Sophie Jackson."

"I like it." I grinned, and I really did. I liked her. She had this magnetism about her that made me want to get closer, made me want to touch, taste, smell.

She held up her plastic cup and tapped it against mine. "I guess I'll see you around Knox Tate."

"You're leaving me already?" I put a hand to my chest and faked being heartbroken.

She threw her head back and laughed.

Both Finn and Leo joined me and raked their gazes up and down.

"Mmm… looks like you have enough people to keep you company." She eyed them both.

"Keep us all company," Leo piped up. "Trust me, we're good for it."

"Eh, I'm a one-guy kinda girl."

Finn sighed. "Then I guess we're out. Have fun with the sexy one."

They left us.

The music slowed. "One dance." Was I begging?

She downed the rest of the beer. "One dance."

We linked hands and started swaying slowly. I could taste the beer on her breath, smell the sweet sweat on her skin as her body moved against mine, our hands intertwined. I leaned in and kissed her neck, and she let me. I was so shocked, I did it again to make sure I wasn't hallucinating.

Then she was wrapping her arms around my neck.

And as I looked into her crystal blue eyes, I knew. I would be gone for this girl, and I would love every fucking minute of it.

"Sophie Jackson." I whispered her name, measured it across my tongue, kept it in my soul. "I think I just fell in love."

She didn't laugh.

She just held on to me tighter as if it was true.

And my heart beat a little bit faster.

And I fell a little bit harder.

"Hey." Finn knocked me on the head. "You okay? You look lost."

I shook my head a bit and grabbed more beer. "Yeah, yeah. Hey, let's get shit-faced."

He eyed me tentatively. "You don't get shit-faced — Correction, *we* don't get shit-faced. Last time, poor Leo almost got pregnant."

Leo flipped us both off.

I joined in their laughter because I had to, because if I

didn't, I was afraid I would do the opposite.

I gulped down another beer, well on my way to being buzzed, when I scanned the crowd again and saw Shawn walk in with one of her teammates, Alexa. It was my business to know everyone.

The hell was she doing here?

I'd told her to go to bed!

I slammed the cup down on the table and marched over to her. "You don't belong here."

Her mouth dropped open. "I'm sorry, what?"

Alexa's eyes widened as if one of us was about to throw down.

"You—" I pointed to the door. "—need to leave."

"What crawled up your studious ass and died?" Shawn snorted at me. "I'm here because my friend invited me. I was perfectly happy in my sweats, getting ready for bed when she texted."

And just like that, I was checking out her leather skirt and short white crop top that made me want to devour her whole and come back for seconds, thirds, fourths— There was no end to the tasting I would do.

"You're dressed… inappropriately." Yeah, that's all I had. Maybe I was already drunk, because it came out almost like a stutter, which I'd never done in my entire life, not even when I was getting laid as a freshman in high school by the senior homecoming queen.

Alexa looked between the two of us, snapped her gum, and patted Shawn on the shoulder. "I'll just go get us some beer. You wait here."

Shawn crossed her arms in a protective stance.

Shit, how tall are those heels? And why the hell am I sweating?

"Are you drunk?" she asked.

"Not yet." Not enough, never enough.

"Oh good, so you have plans for public drunkenness. Great." She grinned. "Well, try not to puke in your backpack before the tutoring session tomorrow afternoon."

I glared. "I can hold my alcohol, but thanks."

She just waved me off and walked by like I wasn't fucking Knox Tate.

Again.

Leo and Finn both flashed me dumb-ass grins while students standing around us looked ready to tweet every single individual on their profile with the hashtag #royallybitchslapped.

"Twice." Leo came up behind me. "That's twice she's blown you off."

"I can count. Thanks, though." I was barely keeping myself in control when I noticed Finn talking to Shawn across the room. She was laughing as if he was the funniest idiot on the planet, and when she stopped laughing, she glanced up and flipped me off.

"Oh shit," Leo said under his breath. "He's bringing his A-game, isn't he?"

I glared. "Let him have her."

"How noble of you." Leo grinned. "One would think you're actually… jealous."

"I don't get jealous," I muttered, sucking air from an empty cup only to find out I needed a refill.

"Says the guy drinking cheap beer like it's water." Leo gave me a new cup.

I took it and watched them, staring like a man insane. What the hell was it about her?

Nothing. She was beautiful.

But I saw beautiful on a daily basis.

Maybe it was her attitude.

The way she seemed so hell-bent on not falling for it, falling for us; the way she judged me when any other girl would bend over backward just for a taste of my mouth.

Finn and Shawn started dancing, but soon she bowed out and left Alexa with him. Finn didn't seem to mind though, as he grabbed Alexa by the waist and pulled her close. The girl seemed ready to combust with excitement. And my eyes, my eyes roamed until they landed on Shawn.

She was in line for the bathroom.

Yeah, good luck with that.

I marched over to her, grabbed her hand, and drug her through the lines of people, despite her angry protests, until we were near the stairs. Then we ducked under the caution tape, and I knocked on the upstairs bathroom door, shoved her in, and guarded it like a dog.

She was in there all of two minutes.

Then the door opened. Her eyes narrowed in on me. "You need to pick."

"Pick?"

"Yeah, I don't do this whole hot-cold thing. It's not sexy on TV. It's not sexy now. I don't like assholes, and I don't like guys who are so inwardly confused that they lash out at other people. So, I'm letting you choose. Are you going to be an asshole or a friend?"

"I don't…" I was too surprised to form words. Instead, I burst out laughing. Yeah, the beer was starting to hit. "I don't have friends who are girls."

"Maybe you should try. Might be good for you." She winked. "Plus, I'm a pretty good friend. Just ask Slater."

"Let's leave your roommate out of this."

"Ah, because you hate each other?"

I looked away. "Something like that."

"Uh-huh. All right, I'm waiting then. What will it be?"

I grinned. "Friends means I can't kiss you."

"Exactly." She looked triumphant.

"Hmm…" I tapped my chin then moved closer and trapped her against the wall, my hands on either side of her. I pressed in. "…let me think about it for ten seconds."

"Ten seconds, huh?" She grinned wide. "All right, one—"

I swept down, tasting the two on her lips, followed by the three, four, five. I tasted each number as if she was speaking it against me, like they were a drug. I craved more. I sucked on her tongue and pressed mine against hers in an act of dominance then I ran my hands up and down her ribs.

"Nine."

I groaned as she melted under my touch.

Fuck. "Ten."

"Friends," I said breathlessly. "I think that will work out just great, don't you?"

Her swollen lips parted as she dumbly nodded her head and said in a much more confident voice than I thought she'd have, "Yeah, sure, sounds great. Friends."

"Super." I licked my lips, still tasting her there, and closed my eyes so she wouldn't see the truth in my eyes, or my reaction. Hell, anyone could see my reaction if they just looked down; even tight jeans couldn't hold me back.

Her cheeks went bright pink before she ducked under my arm.

I fell in to step beside her. "So, friend, should we get a drink?"

She looped her arm in mine. "Only if it's not cheap beer."

It was so familiar. The situation the same.

The girl different.

The hair on the back of my arms stood on end when I looked toward the door and saw Slater's look of disgust before he turned on his heel and walked away.

Hell.

It was different.

It had to be.

Because nobody could survive that twice.

Especially not a guy like me.

"Yeah…" I shook off the bad feeling. "…let's go into the kitchen."

I wrapped an arm protectively around her while girls around me pouted as if they'd just lost, which in a way they had.

Guys checked her out even more.

And I was suddenly thankful that I had Leo and Finn to surround us, to encircle and protect her when I couldn't.

Because I knew something she didn't.

Being my friend?

It wasn't good for her.

It was bad.

But I couldn't stay away.

So, I would take what I could get.

"Shower Girl!" Leo shouted and pulled her in for a hug. "How's my second most favorite person on the planet?"

"Thirsty." She winked.

"Atta girl! Don't worry, you've got us watching out for you. We'll keep you safe."

The sentence hung between the three of us like a fucking curse because we all knew, when it had really counted…

We'd failed.

Chapter Sixteen

Shawn

As per their promise, I only had a few drinks and Alexa and I made it home safely; only after she'd left for her own suite did I discover that my roommate had officially locked me out.

I banged on the door.

Then stomped my foot.

I'd forgotten my keys and texted Slater to leave the door open for me. *What part of open did he not understand?*

I tried again.

Leo and Finn were already walking into the suite. Leo pulled out his keys as they shuffled by, yawning loudly, while I was ready to break the door in half with my bare hands if need be.

"Locked out?" Knox said from behind me.

"Yes," I growled. Then I called out, "Slater, you're dead to me!"

Nothing.

Knox sighed and put his hands on my shoulders. They felt heavy as he steered me away from my own door and toward his.

"No, no, no, no, nope!" I dug my heels in. "I'm not sleeping with any of you. I don't even care if it's a friendly sleep. Not happening."

"Cuddle-bug." Leo winked when Knox forced me into the room. "There's room for two." He pulled back his white duvet.

I made a face.

He actually looked hurt.

Either that, or he was still slightly drunk.

"Take my bed." Knox pointed. "I'll sleep on the floor."

Finn and Leo's eyebrows both shot up to their foreheads at alarming rates.

"No." I scratched my head. "I can take the floor. No problem. Actually, I can sleep out in the—"

Knox covered my mouth with his hand. "Take the bed. I just washed the sheets yesterday. Sleep."

And that was it.

He was already grabbing a pillow and blankets and putting them on the floor. Then the lights were off.

I was still gripping my cell like a lifeline, fully clothed in the middle of what felt like a seriously intense male harem.

"Um…" I swallowed my nervousness. "…all right."

I flipped off my shoes, crawled into nice cool sheets that held a hint of fresh-scented laundry soap and a bit of Knox's spice then slowly pulled my skirt off. I kept my top on and laid my head against his pillow.

It was nice.

Comfortable.

I kind of wanted to steal his bed and give him mine.

What kind of college student had this type of sheets? The thread count had to be insanely high.

Maybe he was rich. Probably was. He drove a nice Mercedes, and I'd noticed the Rolex earlier. *Hmm*. I decided since we were friends I could probably ask him without sounding offensive. Then again, it seemed weird.

I yawned and succumbed to exhaustion just about the time I heard Knox's voice mutter, *"She's dead."*

I slept soundly for about two hours but was pulled awake by the sound of someone tossing and turning then more whispering and soft moans. I looked over the edge of the bed. Knox was battling demons in his sleep, gripping the sheets as if they were his sword and looking so pained my heart clenched.

"Knox," I whispered, touching his side. "Knox."

His eyes jolted open as he jerked to a sitting position. He ran his hands through his long hair.

"Are you okay?"

"Yeah." His eyes were wide, his skin pale, even in the ambient light. "Yeah, I'm fine."

He was shaking.

I wasn't stupid.

A grown man shaking was not a small thing.

I would regret it later — my heart knew it — but I was a caretaker by nature, so when I grabbed his hand and gave it a tug toward the bed, I was surprised he followed.

Even more surprised that when he joined me in his bed, he didn't try to pull me into his embrace; he didn't even touch me, just laid there and stared up at the ceiling like the monsters were going to come back.

"You need to sleep," I whispered, turning on my side and

facing him. "Or you'll be even grumpier in the morning."

He smiled at that. "Am I really that grumpy?"

"Scale of one to ten?" I shrugged. "You flirt with an eight or nine on a good day."

"Shit." He took a deep breath. "For the record, I'm sorry."

"For?"

"Being myself." He didn't offer any more explanation. Instead, he turned away from me, tucked a pillow under his head, and slept.

We were strangers.

And still, when I woke up with the bed empty...

I realized.

It was the second time I'd slept through the night since transferring. Ironic that it would happen to occur in my enemy's bed.

Chapter Seventeen

Shawn

SLATER WAS GONE by the time I made it back to my room, which was rare for him to leave so early. I was tempted to short sheet his bed or do something equally stupid just to teach him a lesson, but I didn't have time before my next weightlifting session. I changed into a tank top and some black Nike tights then laced up my pink shoes and donned my white hoodie.

I almost ran right in to Finn when I opened the door. "Holy crap." It took a couple of deep breaths for my heart rate to return to normal.

He grinned. "Sorry."

"Warn a girl next time."

"Panthers never warn their prey." He grinned shamelessly.

I just rolled my eyes. "What's up?"

He nodded toward the door. "I'm headed to the gym. Let me give you a ride."

"Really?" I perked up. I hated being late because Coach loved making me do weighted wall sits. "Actually, that would be great."

"Thought you might be excited to get there on time."

"Yeah okay, stalker."

He didn't deny it, just laughed.

We made our way down to the lobby. A brand new black SUV was parked in front. He walked to the driver's side while I frowned.

"Something wrong?" He put on his black sunglasses, making him look like a movie star.

"No." I opened my door and got in. "How much do people pay you guys? I mean, each of you has such nice cars."

"Remember? I'm a child star." He winked. "Leo drives a Jetta because he says it makes him look more human." His long sigh was noted. "And Knox? Well, Knox is kind of our leader, if you will. He gets a bigger cut, and he's being groomed for corporate. They basically spoon-feed him gold while he shits diamonds."

"Seriously?"

"He's the best out of the three of us, always has been, always will be. Plus, he has a nice fancy VP position just waiting for him when he graduates. That's part of what we do. We're glorified interns. We put in the blood, sweat, and tears, and hopefully at the end of our senior year, we get a corner office and a yacht."

"You're joking."

He just shrugged. "At any rate, Leo and I have another year because we fucked around too much our freshman year, while Knox is almost done serving time. That's why we were trying to recruit Chris and Jay."

I frowned. "They don't have the same charisma you guys

have."

"Thanks, cupcake." He patted my leg then squeezed my thigh. "It takes time. Confidence isn't earned. It's learned. And we've had time, and epic fails, behind all of ours."

"Fails?" I asked, just as he pulled up to the gym and cut the engine.

Finn turned to me, his gaze just as penetrating as before. "Not really my story to tell. Just know, it hasn't always been raining cash and glory on us three... and there's a reason we're training two more guys, not one, to take Knox's place."

I narrowed my eyes, searching for clues in his gaze. "Because it takes two to replace one so good?"

"Nope." He opened his door and looked over his shoulder. "Because the rules state we need four people."

"So, where's the fourth guy now?"

He swallowed hard then whispered, "You're living with him."

I had figured as much, but hearing it was still jarring. "What happened?"

"Storytime is officially over." He checked his watch. "Hurry up so you won't have to do wall sits."

I rolled my eyes and grabbed my bag. "Your stalker skills are a bit scary."

"It's my job to know things."

"I can tell." I gave him a quick side hug. "Thanks for the ride."

"Anytime, Shawn."

It was the first time he'd said my name, and when he took off his sunglasses and locked eyes with me, it wasn't lust or sex I saw in their depths.

No, it was something much more dangerous.

It was hope.

Chapter Eighteen

Knox

CLASSES SUCKED.

I felt like an absolute ass ignoring every single girl who glanced my way, but I just wasn't into it today. It was my job to lure them in, to be unobtainable, to give them dreams about what it would be like to grab my hair and pull.

And yet there I was, done with class, sitting at the coffee shop like a chick, waiting to see if Shawn would show up like Finn said she would.

The guy knew her schedule backward and forward. I once asked him how he got so much information on every person on the planet. He'd just shrugged and said he had people.

My ass.

The guy would do wonders for Wingman, Inc. once he graduated. I knew part of the reason they liked him was because of his genius.

I played with the lid of my coffee cup and suddenly felt it.

The anger.

It swirled around me.

Slowly, I looked up into Slater's dark gaze.

"So now you speak to me?" I hadn't meant to sound like such a dick.

He took a seat, his eyes never wavering from mine. It was a stare down of epic proportions.

And the shitty part was that the entire school was going to be talking about it in the morning. Our shit was legendary.

I was surprised that Shawn was still in the dark, or maybe she just pretended to be in the dark, because Slater? He was a good actor. He joked. Then again, that had been his job back in the day, right?

He joked; he teased; he was safe.

So fucking safe.

The girls loved him. The guys wanted him.

And he'd primed every single client to perfection. It had been almost too easy when it was the four of us.

"I'm only going to say this once," he rasped.

"I'm listening." I leaned back and crossed my arms.

He glared. "Stay the fuck away from her."

My eyebrows shot up, even though I wasn't all that surprised. "The *her* being your roommate?"

"Yeah, the girl whose throat you had your tongue down last night. That girl." He curled his lip into a sneer. "But now that I think about it, you always had a shitty memory. Need me to draw you a picture?"

"That's enough," I said through clenched teeth. "Don't want you to make a scene. I know how you hate those."

He looked ready to explode, fists clenched, eyes full of

rage. I could feel it then, feel the hurt mixing its way in, the injustice.

It pulled the air from my lungs.

It made me sick to my stomach.

"She's innocent," Slater said in a hushed tone. "Keep her that way."

I nodded, agreeing with him even though I hated every second of it. "We're just friends. I promise."

"And the kiss?"

"Trust me. It won't happen again. I gave my word."

"It's funny you think your word actually means something. Funny how I seem to remember a similar conversation with you a few years back, and yet here we fucking sit."

"Sophie wasn't—"

"Don't," he hissed. "Don't say her name. Just. Don't."

Tears welled in his eyes.

I looked away. I had to.

I couldn't handle the pain I saw there, or the way it made me want to slit my own wrists so he could see that I still bled for her, still missed her, still hated myself for what happened to her.

He stood. "I mean it, Knox. You owe me."

"I know," I whispered. "I know."

He walked off, leaving gaping students staring at me and him, probably mentally calculating how long it had been since we'd been in the same room.

Easy.

Her funeral.

Chapter Nineteen

Shawn

Knox was late to our tutoring session, and when he did show up, it was without textbook, meaning we had to share, and no coffee. Not that I minded, but he just seemed... different since last night.

He was all business.

From the way he sat a few feet away from me to the way he didn't meet my eyes when helping me outline.

An hour went by where he didn't smile, or tease, or flirt, and I found myself missing it.

This Knox? The one sitting next to me? I didn't recognize him. "Everything okay?"

He sighed. "Yeah, just tired."

I winced. "My fault. Hopefully, Slater will be in a better mood tonight and actually let me in the room, though, just in case, I have my keys—"

"He will be," he said in a confident tone.

"And you know the future now?"

He flinched as if I'd slapped him. Then he leaned back in his chair. "Something like that." He checked his watch. "Why don't you finish outlining that last page the way I showed you. I have… a client."

"Oh." I pasted on a smile, but I wasn't feeling it. My cheeks tightened with the need to keep it firmly in place. "Okay, thanks again."

He stared at me for a few brief seconds before grabbing his bag and walking out the door without a backward glance.

Something was definitely off, but I didn't have time to process. I had work to do. I kept working on the outline and was about two paragraphs in when I heard the whispers, felt the stares and points.

I looked up.

People were taking pictures of me on their phones.

Others were whispering and laughing.

What had I missed?

As calmly as possible, I grabbed my stuff, shoved it in my backpack, and made my way out of the library.

Leo was in front. "Ready?"

"Huh?"

He shoved his hands in the pocket of his jeans. "Knox said you had a few more things to write down, so I was waiting."

"For what?"

He frowned. "To drive you back to the dorms."

"But why?"

"Because you shouldn't have to walk when you have three chivalrous gentlemen willing to give you a ride." He winked.

"I bet you've been waiting all day to use that double entendre."

"Two days." He held up two fingers. "Now get in the car, Shower Girl. It's time to go back to the dorm and cheer up your grumpy roommate."

"Don't you mean yours?" I snorted.

"Knox is always grumpy. What else is new?"

But why?

I would also peg him as tortured, confused, and a bit too confident in his sexual abilities.

It bothered me.

I hated that I wanted to figure him out, and I wondered if that was all part of the plan with Knox. Did he tie everyone up in knots? Is that how he got people sucked in to his vortex of moaning and orgasms?

I shivered.

"Chilled?" Leo grinned. "You know a nice hot shower might be in order…"

"Alone," I clarified. "And maybe."

"What if you trip?" He pulled down the street and parked in front of our dorm. "I don't think I could live with myself if anything—" His face paled then he wiped a hand down it as if he'd just said something stupid, like he'd just messed up or committed a crime.

I reached out and touched his arm. "Hey, everything all right?"

His smile was forced. It was the first time I'd noticed that he looked older, more mature than a junior in college, like life had knocked him around a bit.

"Yeah, it has to be, right?"

"Right." My eyes narrowed. "You know, you don't have to do the thing around me."

He cut the engine and turned his full attention to me. "The thing?"

"Yeah." I unbuckled my seatbelt. "The 'hey, I'm so sexy it's hard to keep clothes on, oh, let me touch you just once and stare through you like I'm making love to your soul' thing." I shrugged then yawned. I was too tired to help my bad manners. "It's just me. I'm not a client. You don't have to do it."

His expression sobered.

And he looked away from me like I had just offended him.

I reached for him. "I'm sorry. I didn't mean—"

"Yeah, you did. You meant every word. Do you think this is an act? Some sort of practiced sexual persona that I have to put on each day like my fucking pants?"

"Uh…" I swallowed against the dryness in my throat. "…no?"

He leaned in until our faces were about a half inch apart; his gaze pinned mine. "What would you say if I told you it took me two hundred and six days to figure out just the right amount of pressure to use against a woman's mouth?" He tilted his head. "Or the precise moment when a body begs to be touched? Would you believe me? Or say I was full of shit?"

"Both." I grinned.

He returned my smile. "Thanks for the offer, but honestly, Shower Girl, I don't know how to be that guy anymore."

"What guy?"

"The one before her," he whispered then kissed me on the cheek. "But thank you for believing I could be."

"I never said—"

"You didn't have to. It's in your eyes… I like it, you know. I like the faith you have in me, Finn, especially in Knox. I like that you see past the shit. The problem with that is we're so deep in it, the only one who doesn't realize it isn't real is Knox, and that's because he's too busy punishing himself."

"Why would he do that?"

Leo opened his car door and said over his shoulder, "We all deal with pain in different ways. Some of us walk through it, some let it consume them, and others? They let it play on repeat. It's called eternal punishment. Hell."

Chapter Twenty

Knox

I COULDN'T SIT next to her and not touch her. It had never been a problem before, and now? Now it just made me that much more eager to touch her. But Slater's eyes… his face…

I squeezed my eyes shut.

Leo had brought her back to the dorm, but she'd left a few hours after that with a friend I didn't recognize, which made me even more paranoid.

And that was how I ended up across the street from the club.

Sipping fucking green tea and watching the red door like someone who should have a restraining order strapped to his chest.

She'd been in there for two hours.

Hadn't left yet.

But also wasn't answering her phone.

As her TA, I had her number.

As her friend, she'd never given it to me.

Probably smart.

I had a thing about seeing my name on girls' phones. I shuddered and tried to push the memory away as my stomach clenched, but it was too strong.

"Your name!" Slater shouted. "It was your name on that screen! YOU DID THIS!" he roared, throwing the first punch as the police tried to separate us.

As the sound of the coroner zipping up the body bag filled the universe around us.

As my first tear fell.

I tried to shake the memory away. Rein it in. I gritted my teeth and called her cell again. It was close to midnight, a school night. She should be back at the dorm, studying, watching movies, not out partying with God-knew-who from her team.

Finn said he'd only seen blond hair.

Leo had been in the bathroom.

One job. Protect her.

I tossed my tea in the trash then slowly made my way across the street and toward the mocking red door as techno pumped out into the night air. I showed my ID. The burly security guard nodded to me and unhooked the rope. I stepped in, my eyes instantly squinting against the haze of smoke and stage lights. The smell of sweat and nicotine filled the air as bodies ground in a massive wave of soon-to-be one-night stands.

The club was on the small side; it used to be a coffee shop.

The bar stretched out across the left side of the place and

had barstools in a semi-circle around it.

It was two steps up from the rest of the floor, giving a good view of the place. I walked over and sat then started surveying all the drunk people dancing.

Where the hell was she?

Damn it, I needed to put a tracker in her shoe or something.

Yeah, that was just what she needed to find, a tracker in her shoe from the guy she'd never even given her number to, the same guy who had her address and GPA. Great. Awesome.

My eyes were starting to water from the smoke when I saw a flash of mocha skin and breasts.

I tried to pry my eyes away from the breasts.

And failed miserably.

A white dress that looked more like athletic tape barely covered them, and it looked like it was missing a good foot from the bottom. If she tripped, she was going to get arrested for public nudity.

"Hey there," a familiar female voice came from my right.

I barely held my groan in as I slowly turned and eyed Jessica up and down. She was wearing a tight black tank top and black skirt. It was just enough leather to cover tits and ass, but that was it. "Can I help you?"

"Ohh…" She ran a finger lightly down my arm.

I shuddered from the need to brush her off and run.

"I think you have several times already, haven't you?"

"Jessica…" I said her name smoothly, like I was in control when my heart was hammering against my chest with this need to find Shawn and make sure she was safe. "…this isn't the time. Besides, you aren't a client anymore."

"Your kiss said otherwise," she teased with a little lick of her cherry-red lips.

Had I really thought she was passably attractive?

Yeah, she had a banging body, but she was possessive, needy.

All the things she'd reported her ex had said to her before he dumped her ass.

Color me fucking shocked.

"Come on, Knox..." She grinned and walked into my personal bubble, which just pissed me off more. "Let's get out of here."

"I'll tell you what." I eyed the bartender and ordered a beer. Within seconds, I was shoving it in Jessica's hands. "Drink this, and I'll try to make it back before you're finished."

Her eyes lit up.

It was a lie.

But I figured the two guys checking out her ass, flanking either side of her trying to be incognito, would be more than happy to take my place. I gave one of them a wink and tipped her into his arms before saying my goodbye and bolting toward the dance floor.

He was probably sainting me in his head right about now.

And another life changed—or ruined — however you wanted to look at it, since it was Jessica I was giving him, but whatever.

I eyed the dance floor as women started bumping and grinding around me. Somehow, my bun was grabbed, my hair pulled. I was almost stripped out of my leather jacket by the time I made it to Shawn, who was dizzily holding her head in place as if it was going to fall off while people danced around her.

"Hey!" I yelled.

She didn't look up.

I tapped her on the shoulder.

Her pupils were pinpoints.

My body felt weak.

Too similar.

Damn Slater for putting it in my head, for feeding my paranoia in such a horrible way.

Pain sliced through my chest as I gently grabbed her arm and pulled her into the protection of my body, yelling in her ear, "We should get you home."

She nodded, her breath coming out slow as she slurred, "I don't know what happened. I had two drinks, just two…" She was heavy against me.

"You sure?" I heaved her into my arms and walked her to the outskirts of the dance floor. "Did anyone give you a drink?"

She giggled a bit. "Well, yeah, but that's the point… I had a hard day, you know? Because of the texts…"

"Texts?" I repeated. "What texts?"

"About you… and me…"

I smirked. "You and me? What about us?"

"And Leo and Finn." She yawned and patted my chest. "They said I was the new slutty transfer, and there was a picture of us kissing at the frat party then somehow, one of me in Leo's car and—"

Rage filled me, hot and quick. I'd always wondered when it would happen, when someone would get so resentful of us befriending another girl that they'd start shit again.

It's why we kept our SHIT off campus.

Hell.

This was all Leo's and Finn's fault.

And mine.

We'd been so starved for something… anything… maybe even redemption… that we'd taken one look at the challenge in front of us and accepted, without even realizing how hard it would be for her.

"Let's get you in bed first." I carried her to my car amidst her giggles of being taken to bed then being tickled. By the time we were back on campus, she was crying and telling me a story about her favorite cartoon characters.

Teenage Mutant Ninja Turtles.

"It's why I like cheese pizza." She yawned when we got back to the room.

Leo and Finn were already in bed, the lights down low. With a grunt, I picked her up over my shoulder and knocked on her door.

The door jerked open.

Slater took one look at her and cursed. "Really? What part of 'stay away' don't you understand?"

"She was alone at a club with God-knows-who, and I think she was roofied. Want to keep yelling at me or help?"

Slater's face paled. He stumbled backward, the memory obviously too much.

I knew that feeling. I was currently battling it like a fucking demon in my own chest.

"I've got this," I said in a low voice. "Go take my bed. I'll stay up if she needs anything."

"That's not your job." He crossed his arms.

"It isn't yours either," I fired back.

We stared each other down for a few more seconds then he was grabbing that damn unicorn, which I still refused to touch, and stomping across the room. He didn't even knock, just opened up my door while Finn and Leo started cussing for being woken up.

He yelled right back.

They yelled at him some more.

So much yelling.

Then… silence.

I kicked the door shut behind me just as Shawn opened her eyes wide and stumbled to the trash can, puking every part of her insides into the outside.

"What happened?" she asked between heaving. "Two drinks, just two."

"Drugs," I guessed. "Who were you with?"

"A friend—" She heaved again. "Can we talk later when I'm not halfway in the trash can with my ass showing?"

Naturally, I looked right at her ass and had to smile at the fact that she wasn't hysterical, which was what I would have expected, what I was prepared for.

"Yeah, let me grab you some Ibuprofen and Gatorade. You'll need it. Roofies make you feel like you've been run over by a truck."

She groaned louder.

And for some reason, I liked it.

I hated that she was suffering.

But this feeling? The one where I finally got to play hero instead of villain?

Yeah, a starved man could get used to that sort of feasting.

Chapter Twenty-One

Shawn

I'D BEEN DREAMING I was being chased by Slater's stupid unicorn. At one point, it had caught me and tried to bite down on my ankle, only to stop when I told it I had Skittles.

My heart pounded as I jolted awake.

A heavy arm was draped over me.

I knew that arm.

I traced my fingers down the firm muscle toward the massive shoulder it belonged to then ran my hand through dirty blond hair. It should be a crime to have tresses like that and have a penis. His hair was silky and smooth while still being thick.

I stopped moving my hand, but he grabbed it again and placed it against his head as if he wanted more.

"Please…" he murmured.

I sighed and scratched his head then ran my fingers down his neck. His lips parted. I touched them too, because I was curious, because when his eyes were closed, I could almost believe that he didn't realize I was touching every inch of his body out of curiosity, but also out of disbelief. This guy here was too much of all the right things to be real.

"How'd you sleep?" Knox's eyes were still closed as he asked the question.

I sighed against him, not ready to wake up and face the music of last night. "I dreamed that a unicorn was chasing me, and I remember puking out ten pounds of food last night."

"More like twenty," he said in a dry tone.

I smacked him on the chest.

He grabbed my hand and held it tight. This time his eyes were open when he whispered, "Never again."

Shame hit me hard and fast as I ducked my head and licked my lips. "I'm sorry. I don't normally drink, and after the whole social media shitstorm…"

"You think I'm pissed because you drank?" He frowned.

I nodded, feeling worse.

"Drink, party, explore whatever weird sexual fantasies you have with unicorns." His lips twitched, his perfect pout was almost irritating. "Just make sure you have a sober buddy with you, all right? And for the record, I'm more than happy to volunteer for the job."

I scrunched up my nose. "That sounds like the worst job ever for my new friend."

His eyes narrowed. "Why not me?"

"Well, let's see… have my TA follow me around while I explore my sexuality with some random stranger…"

His fists clenched.

"…or do it on my own?"

"Not on your own." He glared. "And I changed my

mind. You aren't exploring anything with anyone, ever."

"Oh?" I smirked. "Gonna lock me in my room or just order a chastity belt from Amazon? Get it Primed right on over?"

His expression clouded. "You think they have one on Amazon Prime?"

I hit him with one of the pillows, which sent me reeling backward onto the ground in a huff.

He grinned down at me. "I think I'd like to see you all suited up… Think of it as an adventure. The day you find the key you can unlock the treasure."

I gave him the finger while he howled with laughter.

"You're impossible," I grumbled. "And I'll find another buddy, maybe Leo or Finn wouldn't mind."

His expression contorted, and he went ape-shit. "The hell you are! If anyone is going with you, it's me!"

"But—" Heat rushed into my cheeks. "—it would be weird."

"Why?"

"Because we're friends," I said in a hollow voice.

Or maybe just because he still intimidates me, and I still taste him on my tongue. Yeah, those reasons too.

Knox sighed. "It doesn't matter anyway. It's not like you're hell-bent on exploring your sexuality. You just had a bad day. Won't happen again."

"Are you asking or telling?"

"It was a one-time thing, right?" His eyes locked onto mine, as if he needed me to agree with every fiber of his body, and I wouldn't have put it past him to log onto his Amazon account and make real on his threat just to prove he meant business.

Bastard.

"You know?" I got up and stretched. "I think I will."

He stood, towering over me. "You got drugged last night."

"I'll be more careful next time."

"Next... time." He said the words slowly as if he was tasting, waiting for the bitterness around them to fill his mouth. "You're impossible!"

He gave me his back.

"Thank you, though, for last night," I said in a small voice. "I'm equal parts embarrassed and ashamed that I was so stupid to take a drink from someone I barely knew. I must have turned around or something. I guess it only takes a few seconds, huh?"

His shoulders relaxed as he slowly turned around. "Seconds, and a life could end. Yes." His eyes were wild. "I want it to be me. I need it to be me, but if you can't get ahold of me, take Leo, Finn — hell, I don't even care if you take Slater. Just make sure you have someone with you. Anything can happen. You're too pretty for your own good."

He thinks I'm pretty! I tried not to smile too wide.

And failed.

He just shook his head and smiled. "I'm impressed with your restraint."

"I have no idea what you're talking about."

He smirked. "Lies." Knox opened the door and called over his shoulder. "The last girl I called pretty passed out into her birthday cake — so yeah, the restraint is admirable, also pretty tempting."

"That's my goal. Tempt you until you can't handle it anymore." I laughed.

He didn't. Instead, he walked tensely across the room, and I could have sworn he said, "It's working."

Chapter Twenty-Two

Knox

I RAN MY hands through my long hair and stood in the middle of the room. A feeling of nostalgia hit me so hard and fast that I had to lean against the wall before I could catch my breath.

Leo and Finn were sleeping with their mouths open.

And Slater?

Slater was spooning the damn unicorn.

Maybe if I was still enough, the universe would right itself again? Maybe she wouldn't be dead. We would all still be friends? Maybe it would be different.

I sighed.

It was enough for Slater to jolt awake; he always was a light sleeper. His green eyes zeroed in on mine. "She okay?" His voice was gravelly from sleep.

I nodded. "She's embarrassed, still swears up and down she only had two drinks. I think someone saw an opportunity and took it."

Slater gritted his teeth.

I knew that look.

He wanted to pummel whoever thought to drug her.

Get in line.

"I, uh, told her she needed a buddy to go with her next time she goes out. You know, like a sober sexless buddy." I added in the sexless part just in case Slater got it in his head he was a suitable candidate.

"Sexless," he repeated. "So, you three are out then? Is that what you're saying?"

Somehow, Finn had picked up on the conversation and held both hands in the air with his middle fingers high.

Leo yawned and said, "My dick's bigger than yours." Then turned over on his side and went back to sleep.

I wondered if he missed it.

Slater looked away then slowly started getting out of my bed. "Thanks for letting me crash and for taking care of her."

Finn was watching us with wide eyes as Slater sidestepped me and went across the hall, dragging his giant unicorn across the carpet with him.

"No bloodshed?" Finn asked out loud. "You sure he wasn't drugged too?"

"Shut it," I groaned. "Both of you pay attention. Shawn needs anything, you give it to her, all right?"

Leo grinned seamlessly.

"Anything but that," I said through clenched teeth. "Look, I like her…" I grumbled. "I mean, we're friends."

If Leo's and Finn's smiles get any bigger, I am tossing them out the window.

"You mean you *like*-like her?" Leo joked.

"He super likes her a bunch," Finn said in a giddy voice.

"Think she'll come play Legos later?"

"Out." I pointed at the door. "Both of you, dead to me."

"Hey, we just like seeing boss man happy." Leo winked. "Don't we, Finn?"

"By Legos, I meant your penis. Sorry if that was confusing." Finn slapped me on the back as he grabbed a towel and his flip-flops. "But seriously, the friend-zone plan only works for so long."

"Come again?" I hissed. "What do you mean the friend-zone plan?"

Finn shook his head. "Don't play dumb. You can only friend-zone for two months before your balls fall off. It's been documented to happen—"

"To Canadians." Leo nodded slowly. "But maybe it's just because they don't have big packages, and all their police are Mounties?" said the actual Canadian of the group. The guy even had a flag on the wall.

I groaned. "It's too early for you two."

Somehow, I was getting led to the chair and pushed into it. The minute my ass hit the seat it rolled backward, only to be stopped by Finn a second later.

"Rule number one." Leo cleared his throat and grabbed the armrests, leaning in. "Be the trustworthy TA, be the friend, friend her so damn hard that when she looks up friendship in the dictionary, it's your face with a heart around it."

"Friend her hard," Finn repeated from behind while Leo placed his hands on my shoulders and continued.

"Once the friendship and trust are established, she'll find it easy to touch you, a light jab here, a playful kick there." He laughed then said in a high-pitched voice, "Knox, you're so funny. Stop it, Knox. That tickles!"

"Are you supposed to sound like the creepier version of Tickle Me Elmo?" I wondered out loud.

Leo slapped me across the face.

I almost broke his wrist.

He winced. "Listen up, it's been a while since you've been in the game, so this is how it's going to go. Eventually, you're going to have a moment somewhere between the touching and the witty banter. The moment's going to feel serious. You're going to start sweating, and that's how you know you need to go for it. That's her sign, man. The universe's tell that she's ready for more than the friend-zoning."

I gulped. "You guys are acting like I don't already know this shit."

"Oh, you know it, but can you actually handle it?" Leo rolled his eyes. "We do this shit for a living, but you've never lived it. Good luck out in the wild, my man. You're going to need it."

"I don't need it." I needed it. I needed all of it.

Holy shit, I am already sweating. Is this what normal human guys feel like when they like someone? I've only had it happen once, and it didn't feel this strong.

Which just made the fear that much more real.

"I can't," I whispered. "Not again."

"This is different, and you know it is," Finn said in a serious voice.

I stood. "Maybe." But my mind was already made up.

I'd protect her, I'd be her friend, but that was all I could offer.

That was all I trusted myself with.

Chapter Twenty-Three

Shawn

I FELT SLUGGISH the entire day, and by the time I made it to Human Anatomy, Leo had already saved me a seat and brought coffee. Whatever I'd done in my pitiful life to deserve him, I wanted to do again, especially if he brought me coffee and easy grins that immediately put me at ease.

"Drink up, Shower Girl." Leo shoved the steaming cup under my nose. I inhaled Pike Place Roast and almost moaned out loud.

Leo immediately reached out and rubbed by shoulders with his large hands, making me lean into him helplessly as the professor droned on about something I could care less about but needed to start caring about if I was going to pass the class.

"So," Leo whispered. "You were drugged?"

I sighed as fresh embarrassment washed over me. "Can we not talk about it?"

He shrugged, kneading my shoulders harder before tugging my chair toward his so that our thighs were almost touching. "It helps to talk."

"Ah, how could I forget?" I said under my breath. "You're the talker."

"Well, both Finn and I like to use our words more than our mouths — shocking, I know. Don't ask Knox for words, though. He's all action, that one."

I tried to ignore the butterflies in my belly and the way I suddenly felt both sick and excited all at once. "Yeah. I know."

"Should you talk about it?"

"No." I clammed up. "It was a mistake. I was trying to let off steam. I'll be more careful next time. Promise."

"Next time…" He leaned in until I could feel his warm breath on my neck. "…ask one of us to go with."

I felt my body tense all over again.

"What was that?" He stopped massaging. "Why are you stressed with the thought of one of us hanging out with you? I can hold back hair while you puke, too, you know."

I smiled then put my hands over my heated face. "Don't you guys get paid for that sort of thing?"

"We don't charge our friends," he said thoughtfully. "And I'd like to think that's what we are. After all, I've seen you naked and have yet to get you into bed with me. If that's not friendship, I really don't know what is."

"Chivalrous to the bone, aren't you?" I teased.

He just smiled that easygoing sexy smile as he grabbed my hand and held it, squeezing my fingers like he meant it, as if he really was a friend and not just looking to get me into bed. "That's why the ladies like me. But Shawn?"

I stared at him — really stared at him. "What, Leo?" Every

hint of manipulation I was looking for in his mannerisms, words, his body language, was nowhere to be found.

"It's nice to have friends who care about you. Just accept it. You're kind of stuck with us now."

"And how did that happen, I wonder?"

"I saw you naked in the shower, you saw us pleasing one of the ladies and liked it, and you live in the same suite as we do. Plus, if anyone needs protection from the outside world, it's you."

"I'm offended."

"I know." He grinned. "I like it when you get all crazy-eyed."

"And now I'm crazy."

"Duh, you're hanging out with guys who are paid to pleasure people on a daily basis. You're clearly not sane."

"Then neither are you."

"Guilty as charged." He released my hand and scooted away. "Now, drink your coffee. You look tired as hell."

Friends.

I grinned and took another sip. I hadn't really had good friends at my last school, mainly because academics and sports had taken up all my time, and I hadn't thought I needed friends. I was perfectly fine hanging out with teammates.

But now? Now that I knew what it was like?

I never wanted to let the feeling go.

The warm fuzzies of knowing I had people who cared about me for whatever crazy reasons they had, ones who would drop anything to make sure I was okay, safe.

When class finally ended, Leo grabbed my bag like the gentleman he was, and walked me out of class, much to the obvious irritation of the female population. And when Knox met us at the door and did a weird messenger-bag exchange like they were the Secret Service to the President's daughter, I just followed without complaining.

Leo winked. "Have fun studying, kiddos."

Knox groaned and eyed me up and down before clearing his throat and looking away. "Feeling better?"

"Yeah, Leo gave me the best back massage."

He stumbled a bit.

"Are you okay?"

"Perfect," he said through clenched teeth.

"Knox! Shawn!" Finn jogged toward us, two coffees in hand. "Thought I'd catch you before you started studying. Mind if I join you?"

"No," I said at the same time Knox said, "Yes."

Finn just winked and looped his arm in mine. "Thanks, sexy. I brought you coffee 'cuz Leo said you were still tired."

I sighed and leaned into him. "You're the best."

"I know," his answer.

Chapter Twenty-Four

Knox

TWO PENCILS…

One marker — *I know, I know.*

And three pieces of gum later…

And I was still about one minute away from ending Finn's life. I even had seven different ways I could stab him with my pen, all of them vividly graphic and life-ending.

Because he was flirting.

Turning it the hell on.

And making her laugh.

I was sitting right there, yet he commanded every second of her attention. Each time I gave her an assignment or words to study, he'd lean over and find something funny to say that had her throwing her head back and giggling so loud we were getting stares from people around the room.

Not that I minded.

I wanted them to know she was with me.

But not *us*.

Not him.

I wrote *STOP* on a Post-It, folded it, and flung it at his face when Shawn started her next notecard.

He picked it up, read it, and then ripped it slowly into thirds.

Fine.

I grabbed my phone.

> **Knox:** *Team meeting.*
>
> **Leo:** *What up?*
>
> **Finn:** *Knox's jealousy is showing.*
>
> **Leo:** *So it's working?*
>
> **Knox:** *Come again?*
>
> **Finn:** *You need to come at least once before you can come again, amateur.*
>
> **Knox:** *You have two seconds before this pen ends up in your jugular.*
>
> **Leo:** *Damn it. I wish I didn't have calculus right now.*
>
> **Finn:** *He's turning red.*

I clutched my hands into fists, released them, and typed again.

> **Knox:** *Out with it, now.*
>
> **Leo:** *You like her. A lot. And with the pace you've been trying to seduce her, you'll be eighty before you can cop a feel, and nobody wants to see that dude. Nobody.*

> **Finn:** *Agreed. Saggy boobs are still boobs, but why wait that long?*
>
> **Leo:** *If he has a boner right now at the thought of it, the friend-zone really is getting to him.*

Finn scooted his chair and stared at my crotch.

I gave him the finger and blocked myself from view as I adjusted my pants. Damn it. Just talking about it...

Just sitting next to her...

It was physical.

Nothing more.

It was the mixture of her perfume, and her sassy attitude, and that hair. God, her hair was so damn pretty.

I was staring.

Finn coughed.

I looked back down at my phone.

> **Leo:** *Finn said you were just staring at her with your mouth open. Show some decorum. You're better than that shit.*
>
> **Knox:** *What did you guys do?!*
>
> **Leo:** *We're reverse-reverse hareming you.*
>
> **Knox:** *Huh?*
>
> **Finn:** *This is what it's like when other girls see us with clients. They get insanely jealous, break up with their boyfriends, and hop on for a very non-sexual ride. We're making you want her even more than you already do. And from the looks of it, you're like two minutes away from snapping.*
>
> **Leo:** *I say one.*

Knox: *Could you guys just leave it?*

Finn: *True friendship means you deserve true happiness. You took the fall for everyone freshman year. You deserve to be happy, man.*

I looked away from the screen and took a moment to ride out the hurt.

Knox: *I don't want to talk about it.*

Leo: *All right, Finn. Time for Stage 2.*

Finn: *On it.*

The text messages stopped.

Finn dropped his phone onto the table then leaned in to Shawn. "Hey, you should come over tonight."

Shawn smiled but was still writing on her notecard. "You mean make the long trek across the living room?"

"Aw, baby, if it's that long, I can give you a piggyback ride. Just let me know what time to pick you up."

I rolled my eyes.

She laughed. *Is she really buying his shit?*

"I can walk." She shook her head and highlighted the few phrases on her card. "What's the occasion?"

"Friend Day," Finn announced, making me want to drown myself in the nearest cooler of water. "We'll watch movies, eat junk food, you can even invite Slater if he promises to leave the unicorn in his bed."

I tensed.

She frowned. "He's actually gone tonight and tomorrow, something about going to visit his parents."

I tensed even further.

His parents.

I saw two once-laughing individuals.

And then no more smiles.

Just tears.

"Good." Finn's smile became tense and forced. I could tell he was thinking about it too. "What do you say to eight?"

"Count me in." She smiled up at him.

"Perfect." He stood, grabbed his bag, and left.

Thank God.

I was just opening my mouth when Shawn checked her watch. "Shoot, I have practice. Do you think we can finish up tonight?"

"Uh…" I almost stuttered. "…yeah."

"Thanks, Knox." She leaned down and touched my shoulder.

My. Shoulder.

Then gathered her stuff and walked off.

My phone buzzed.

> **Finn:** *Trainwreck: See Knox Tate*
>
> **Me:** *Ex-best-friends: See both Leo and Finn; see also dickwads.*

Chapter Twenty-Five

Shawn

I wasn't sure how to explain it. And the problem was I didn't really have anyone to explain it to. It's not like I could call up Mom and Dad and be like, *"So there's these three guys…*

"No, not one.

"Three.

"Oh yeah, and they're basically like glorified massage therapists without the sexual happy ending but more of moan-filled The End.

"No sex though, so don't worry! Ha ha.

"Oh, and they won't leave me alone.

"And I like one more than the others.

"But I want to keep the others around.

"But like, not in a sexual way."

Yeah, that sounded good.

Like a totally normal conversation to have with one's parents, right? Especially after transferring schools and already complaining to them about classes and lack of friends, not to mention the asshole ex-boyfriend.

I highly doubted they wanted me to go in this direction.

A bit severe.

I chewed my bottom lip and stared across the room at Slater's bed. The unicorn was gone, and he'd left a note with instructions on what creams to use on my face so I didn't *"wake up looking like a zombie."*

I texted Alexa to come over for movie-night, but she wasn't feeling well.

So that left my new friend, Skylar, the same one who had abandoned me the night I'd somehow gotten drugged. Then again, her boyfriend had shown up, and things had gotten heated, so I didn't blame her. Plus, the music had been so loud I'd just wanted to dance and escape it all.

I shuddered. Never again, at least not with someone I barely knew from a team I'd just joined.

It was close to eight.

But I'd seen a girl my age walk into the guys' room a half hour ago, so I wasn't sure if we were still on.

To be safe, I poked my head out the door.

The lights were low.

I held my breath and listened. No sound of moaning.

I made my way across the room and knocked.

Leo answered on the first knock, shirtless. Big shock there. "Almost done, come on in."

"I, uh—"

He jerked me past the doorframe and slammed the door behind him. The room was dimly lit, a few candles were scattered around the desks, and the smell of lavender filled the room.

The girl had something covering her eyes, and her head

was in Knox's lap while Finn rubbed her feet and legs.

"Now…" Finn's deep voice filled the air. "…tell us about what you miss."

"I miss—" Her voice cracked. "—things like this."

"I completely understand." Leo knelt in front of her body and caressed her lips with his fingertips. "You miss the touching, the intimate moments that you're afraid you won't ever get again."

She sighed. Her lips pressed together as if she was trying to keep her cry in.

"Sometimes…" Knox's voice made my body so aware of his presence I couldn't drag my gaze from his even if I'd tried.

His blue eyes locked on to mine. His hair hung around his chin like some old Viking just ready to conquer and pillage every woman in his path. Because that was what Vikings did, right? His lips quirked into a tiny smile as he ran his hand through her long dark hair.

"…sometimes it's better to understand what we miss so we can figure out what we want for our next partner. What you crave is physical attention and someone to listen to you. Those are good things to have in a healthy relationship. What's not healthy is wishing for what could have been."

"Yeah." Her voice was small.

Finn stopped rubbing her feet and gently set them on the floor while Knox helped her stand.

"Rest your head against my chest," Knox whispered, pulling her shoulders gently toward him.

She leaned her body back while Finn approached and, very gently, pressed his lips against hers. She didn't seem to kiss him back, just let him explore.

When he was done, Leo stepped in and kissed her on the cheeks.

And then Knox turned her in his arms and kissed just below her right ear and whispered, "He's an idiot to let you go, but you'll be an even bigger idiot if you pine for him when you could have it all."

He pulled the blindfold from her face. "Do you?"

"Do I what?"

"Want it all?" He tilted her chin toward him.

She nodded.

"Then take it," he encouraged and stepped away just as Leo turned the lights on.

With tears in her eyes, she reached for Knox's hand, squeezed it, and then gave each guy a hug, not even acknowledging that I was in the room.

When the door clicked shut behind her, the guys all gave a collective sigh, as if signaling the work day was finally over.

"Does it emotionally drain you?" I wondered out loud.

Knox was the first to answer, "Every damn time."

"You can't—" Finn broke off with a grimace, only to start again. "—you can't feed someone emotionally without emptying your own tank, Shower Girl."

I frowned and sat on the empty chair in front of one of the desks. "Then how do you fill your tank back up?"

Finn smiled shamelessly along with Leo.

Knox just scowled harder.

"Some of us get it elsewhere… from each other, friends, girlfriends, one-night stands. You can't just get it from one place. But you do need to get it. Got it?"

I narrowed my eyes.

"Finn has one-night stands on a weekly basis," Leo pointed out. "I tend to like the weekends better, but that's when Finn studies. And Knox? Well, Knox hasn't had sex in three years."

Knox groaned and pinched the bridge of his nose.

"I mean, we're not even sure he's had his V taken." Leo nodded seriously.

Knox threw a pillow in Leo's direction.

"Rumor has it that the day he cuts his hair," Finn said in a reverent voice, "will be the day he's met his Delilah, his love, but also his downfall." He snapped his fingers. "Hey, you're good with sharp objects, aren't you, Shawn?"

I laughed and felt instantly sorry for Knox.

"So, enough about me." Knox cleared his throat. "What's your story? Lonely transfer with a very masculine name, set up with Slater, of all people…"

"Eh, what the hell," I muttered. "I'd put every ounce of energy into sports and studying, refused to even go out because it could mess with my nutrition and my game, got to the point where I was losing too much weight and nothing was fun anymore. Let's just say going through serious seasons of depression isn't fun. I'm still on a light medication." I gulped. "And you know, ex-boyfriend— Apparently, my skin color was a factor. Who knew? Sorry I got a bit serious with you guys, but I promised my parents that if I could transfer, I'd try, you know, the whole fresh-start thing. But practice has been killing me, and my classes are a lot harder than I thought. Slater was the first real friend I made next to Alexa. That's kind of why…" Warmth flooded my face. "… why I went out the other night when another girl invited me. I just— I don't want to be that girl anymore, the one who says no then spends the night in her dorm depressed and falling asleep at eight to *Friends*."

All three guys stared at me with new admiration in their eyes, or at least it felt that way.

Finn cleared his throat. "Knox falls asleep to *Friends*

every night, so I wouldn't worry about being the weird one of the group."

Knox grinned over at me. "That may be true."

"If it makes you feel better," Leo said in a serious voice, "we don't let people in to our little group often — too much jealousy from the ones with ovaries — but you're an athlete, which makes you almost like a dude… with really nice boobs."

"Uh, thanks?" I laughed.

"My pleasure." Leo winked, earning a smack on the chest from Knox, who was standing and making his way over to me.

He held out his hand.

I stared at it first then took it. "Where are we going?"

"We're going to the kitchen so I can teach you how to work the microwave, and if you pass with flying colors, we'll work on tying your shoes."

"Be still my heart," I said0 in a bored tone.

"We'll get the movie ready," Leo called.

The door shut behind us.

Knox released my hand.

I didn't like it, not at all.

His hair was wild around his shoulders still. I wanted to touch it again but restrained myself, just barely.

"So…" I needed to fill the silence with my voice so I didn't do something stupid like ask if I could touch his six-pack. "…is that why you keep your hair long? Waiting for the right scissor-happy woman to stumble into your arms and snip-snip?"

He laughed and looked at me over his shoulder. "It's a rumor, something I love toying with every second I can get. Once I was in class and brought scissors up to my hair.

Two girls next to me let out screams. One passed out. It's a clear sign I'm off the market, apparently, and it's just that traumatic to some of our clients."

"Because they want you?"

"Because the idea is that they think they can have me," he admitted. "Not that it matters. Eventually, they find their match through the app and forget all about me, but it keeps them coming back. Every girl thinks they're the game-changer. None of them are."

It felt like a slap to the face.

I nodded even though my body felt numb.

I hadn't realized he'd moved until he was standing right in front of me, touching my shoulders, dragging me against his chest, and tilting my chin toward his mouth.

Warm lips descended, sending my body into a flurry of excitement and danger as I snaked my arms around his neck.

It should be intimidating, kissing this man.

Instead, it felt right.

We fit.

He moaned into my mouth when I flicked his tongue with mine, and when I tugged his hair, he lifted me by the ass onto the counter, dragging his lips down my neck until he was out of breath, his head inches from my breasts.

"Guys?" Leo opened the door. "Popcorn ready?"

"Almost," Knox barked in a hoarse voice.

I frowned. "You haven't even put it in the microwave."

"So?" He kissed me harder.

He made me forget more than the popcorn; he made me forget about everything but the pressure of his lips, the taste of his mouth, and the way his body heat seemed to make my temperature spike to dangerous levels.

We broke apart when the door opened again.

This time it was Finn. "Dude, if you're going to stay out here and get naked, fine by me, but at least feed us before the show."

My face felt like it had been lit on fire.

Knox grinned as he pressed his palm to my cheek. "So beautiful."

It was the first time someone with that face, that sort of body, that sort of mystery, had ever looked me in the eyes and said something so poetic, so real, that I felt my eyes well with tears.

It was in those moments when you hadn't realized how starved you were for the words that mean something, that a god descended from above and whispered truth into existence, and suddenly, you believed him.

I opened my mouth to say something, but he pressed a finger to my lips and turned around and slowly, painfully, pressed buttons on the microwave, then faced me and crossed his arms. "Any questions?"

"You didn't press start."

"You like pushing buttons. You press start."

I rolled my eyes, hopped down, and hit the button, but I could feel him staring behind me. When I turned, he didn't even try to hide that he was looking at my ass. "Seriously? All of that just to stare a bit?"

"Hell yes, and it worked. I got an extra five seconds in." He smiled wide.

Damn it, he was pretty. So pretty.

"Also?"

"Yeah?"

"Worth it." He pushed away from the counter and then wrapped an arm around my waist. "So glad we decided to be friends."

"You just kissed me."

"I slipped."

"Oh?"

"Yeah, the radiation from the microwave got to me."

"So anytime I stand in front of the microwave—"

"I won't be able to control myself."

"Just microwaves?"

"Trees," he said once the microwave beeped, "air…"

I shoved him and started laughing as he grabbed the bag and kissed me on top of the head.

"…movies…" He kissed near my ear. "…study sessions."

"So just be prepared to get pounced at any time?" I pulled away, searching his eyes.

He just shrugged, opened the popcorn, and tossed a kernel in his mouth. "Guess so."

"You're impossible to figure out."

"Heard you like puzzles," was all he said before opening the door and showing me a spot next to his bed; pillows and blankets were everywhere. I grabbed a bowl and let Knox fill it up then laughed when both Leo and Finn flanked either side of me during the movie.

And didn't even flinch when Knox sat behind me and pulled me into his arms like it was normal.

As if all college women had three guys surrounding her like a celebrity.

Nothing was normal.

And yet, not one part of me felt weird.

So, when Finn started playing with my hair casually… when Leo rubbed my left hand and massaged my stiff fingers…

I didn't think twice.

And as I fell asleep against Knox's chest, I could have

sworn I felt two different sets of lips caress my cheek and one touch my mouth.

Chapter Twenty-Six

Knox

"Do you want me to say told you so?" Leo whispered.

The movie was long over. Shawn was tucked into my arms sleeping soundly. The guys had done their job.

They'd gotten her relaxed.

Which was what she deserved. A moment of just… peace, where she didn't have to worry about someone spiking her drink, or a guy taking advantage of her. We had our reputations, but that was not what we were about.

We protected.

We proved what guys could be like if you gave them a chance.

We were the best of the best, and we were that way for a reason.

Because when you fell from the pedestal, you had no other choice but to brush yourself off and become better.

"No." I finally found my voice as I pushed her hair away

from her cheeks. "I like her."

There. I'd said it out loud.

"Thank God," Finn grumbled. "I thought I was going to have to sleep with her to get you to notice."

I glared at him.

He grinned. "Kidding. You know I love pissing you off."

"Consider me pissed," I ground out through clenched teeth.

"Go be angry by the unicorn. We're all full up here." Leo sighed as if I was the heaviest burden of the bunch. "Seriously, go tuck her into bed and keep your hands to yourself. I doubt Slater would mind if you slept in his bed."

"Slater?" Finn repeated. "He would rip Knox's nuts off and feed them to Horny!"

"Never—" I closed my eyes and pinched the bridge of my nose. "—never utter that sentence again."

Finn waved me off. "Whatever, you knew what I meant."

"Right, that's the problem, ass-face." Leo cleaned up some of the popcorn while I gently lifted Shawn into my arms and started the trek back to her room.

I got her door open and laid her down on her bed, and like a creeper, I watched her sleep for a good ten seconds before realizing that I wasn't just hovering over her like a serial killer, but staring at her like some hormonal teenager. I brushed a kiss across her forehead and started to walk away when her hand shot out and grabbed mine.

I stopped as she sat up, looked at me through sleepy eyelids and tilted her head. "Thank you."

"For the popcorn?"

A smile spread across her face. "Yeah, for the popcorn."

"Who knew it was your kryptonite?" I whispered.

She gulped as her eyes darted to my mouth.

I knew hunger when I saw it.

I also knew mine was reflected in her eyes.

"Be honest. If Slater finds you in here, will he kill you?" she asked, tugging her knees to her chest.

"Yes," I answered seriously. "Just know he's probably going to burn my body rather than bury it."

She smirked. "Noted."

"Sleep tight, Shawn."

I leaned in and kissed her forehead again — I couldn't help it.

I was just pulling away when she asked, "What happened with him?"

"Us," I corrected her. "It was an *us* thing."

"You and him?"

I didn't want to talk about it. "Yeah, something like that. It happened a while ago, but it was enough to alter things."

"Tell me about it?"

"It's not a good bedtime story." Or anytime story. "You need sleep. You have practice in the morning followed by a Human Anatomy quiz."

She rolled her eyes. "Right, okay. Thanks, Dad."

I was on her, straddling her before I could stop myself then my hands were in her hair, and my mouth was sucking on hers like an addict.

She wrapped one arm around my neck and held on while I pressed her back against the mattress. My hands had a mind of their own as they ran up and down her ribs and unhooked the flimsy bra with one brush of my fingers, freeing her breasts.

Mine… all mine.

When those soft wonders of nature spilled over into my hands, my eyes rolled up in my head. I massaged them, getting a fucking palm full of ecstasy. "No wonder Leo didn't shut up about you."

"Huh?"

Her nipples were erect, just begging to be sucked. Her breasts were heavy, high, and tight, so fucking warm I wanted to press my face against them. I squeezed then pressed them together, made them my new personal playground. My body buzzed with intense awareness as I looked down at her skin and mine. Light and dark. It was erotic, a beautiful thing, something I couldn't stop staring at as she arched under my touch.

"You're beautiful," I rasped. "Your skin." My fingertips buzzed with electricity as I ran them over her flesh and watched her reactions to the way I touched her, the way I hovered over her. My entire body felt tight. The way she looked at me... Those light brown eyes focused in, drilled through my self-defenses, my fears — and set up camp in the center of my chest.

"Fuck." I touched my forehead to hers and let out a breath.

She tensed, her eyes searching mine for answers, probably an explanation, a reason why we should do this, a reason we shouldn't.

So many reasons, so many questions, and I couldn't stop staring, couldn't even suck air into my lungs as I watched her chest rise and fall.

"I've never seen anything so gorgeous in my entire life." I ran my hands from her breasts along her ribs then leaned down and took a nipple in my mouth and sucked.

Her body bucked then she was tugging my head to hers. She kissed, she licked, and when I gripped her ass, she fucking bit me on the lip like I was the main course.

I chuckled. "Easy there."

"I'm…" She pulled away, eyes hooded, cheeks pink. "… sensitive… everywhere."

"I love it," I said softly as the tension in the room broke. This wasn't my job. This wasn't Wingman, Inc. This was her. Us. A fresh start. "If my fingers make you squirm, imagine what my mouth can do."

She gaped, her lips parting a bit in what I assumed was shock.

"There." I pressed a kiss to her neck. "There's your bedtime story. Goodnight, Shawn."

I got up and tried to not look so aroused, but I was wearing tight jeans, so every part of me was showing. My length was basically trying to wave at her and beg for an invitation to hop back into her bed and dive under the covers. Lights on.

"Hey, Knox?"

"Yeah?" I grabbed the doorknob and turned around.

She peeled the shirt over her head then tossed the bra to the floor. Completely topless, she angled her head, lazily blinking those big eyes.

My entire body went hard — hot, ready — as I braced myself against the door with white-knuckled hands.

"Thanks, I was going to take it off earlier, but you're such a gentleman and just took care of it for me, huh?" She winked pulling the covers over her body. "Can you get the light?"

"Fuck me." I banged my head against the door at least three times before flicking off the light and whispering, "Do that again, and you'll be screaming my name. Oh, and Shawn? When that happens? The lights stay on."

I slammed the door and made the painful walk of shame

back to my room only to find my roommates with both of their phones pointed at me.

They snapped pictures.

"For the family album." Leo nodded while Finn snapped another.

The hell kind of family album held pictures of my erection? "I hate you both."

"Sweet dreams!" Finn announced. "Or should you go take a nice long, hard — sorry, I meant hot — shower?"

I winced then grabbed my towel and my caddy and made another painful jaunt to the bathroom.

Cold shower it was.

Chapter Twenty-Seven

Shawn

I smiled through practice. It might have had to do with my movie night and with the way it had ended, my mouth pressed against his.

"Wow, someone's happy today," Alexa said, once we hit the showers. "You look ready to float right on out of here."

"Yeah?" I played dumb.

She crossed her arms. "Spill. I haven't talked to you since you and your new tutor—" Her eyebrows shot up. "Is he hot?"

"Yeah." My face heated a bit. "He's also kind of Knox."

"KNOX TATE FROM ACROSS THE SUITE?" She apparently just had to yell.

I covered her mouth with my hand. "Could you not scream it?"

"Sorry." She looked around the emptying locker room and gave me a huge grin. "So, what's he like?"

"What do you mean? He's a great tutor."

"I mean, what's he like, the other... *side* of him."

"The grumpy side?"

Alexa threw up her hands. "You know what I mean!"

I did. But I wanted something for me. Something that wasn't going to be tweeted about or talked about around campus. "He's really great."

"Oh, that's super," she said sarcastically then laughed. "Little tramp."

"Hey, now! It's just studying." And a few stolen kisses... some boob-grabbing... It hurt to keep myself from smiling too big at her.

"Sure it is." She laughed. "We should go out this weekend. Sorry I was gone last weekend, but I'll make it up to you. Maybe you can bring your suitemates, and I can try to get one of them to make me forget my troubles."

Jealousy crept into my body.

And it wasn't just the thought of her and Knox; it was the thought of her and all of them. Like I somehow had a right to three guys instead of one. The others were my friends, yet they were somehow more to me, even though it was Knox I liked.

"Yeah..." I found myself saying slowly. "...I'll ask."

"You're the best!" She twirled then whipped me with her towel. "Now go shower. You smell like a Knox Tate wet dream."

"Ha-ha, very funny." I rolled my eyes while secretly wondering if it was true, if there really was more between us, or if he was just doing what he did.

Made women think they had a chance.

Then got their rocks off and left.

The thought lingered in the back of my mind the rest of the day.

Chapter Twenty-Eight

Knox

She'd come to me.

To. Me.

And asked me to be her sober buddy.

Like we hadn't crossed some stupid invisible line three days ago! I was so pissed I couldn't see straight, and when I didn't answer right away, she'd backed off and said she could always make sure Leo and Finn were free, which had made me start yelling for no reason.

She had stared me down as if I'd grown seven heads and barked, *"My human,"* while tossing her over my shoulder and stomping into my imaginary cave.

"We'll all go," I'd said.

Famous last words.

Because babysitting two athletes with bodies like that?

Let's just say I'd rather be in prison.

And would probably end up there soon if the guys didn't

stop hitting on the girls.

I made sure to give her a glass of water with each drink and babysat her alcohol like she'd never been to a party before.

The girls were two drinks in, dancing with Leo and Finn in the middle of the dance floor, when I felt it. The devil, or maybe just his female minion. She snaked her hands around my chest. I'd recognize those pink talons anywhere.

"What do you want, Jess?"

"Dance with me," she purred. I could smell the gin on her breath and visualize her come-hither glance that many a man had fallen prey to.

"Nah, I'm good."

"I know…" She squeezed my ass.

I clenched my teeth.

This. This is why I hated my job.

They thought they had the right.

Because I'd made them feel good.

I'd made them think they were invincible.

Ninety percent of the time it was perfect.

Jessica was the other ten percent that I wished didn't know our services existed.

"It's late," I said in a bored voice. "You should go home."

"It's midnight."

"Exactly." I shrugged out of her arms and made a beeline toward the middle of the dance floor, jerked my head back so Leo could see who I was talking about, and swapped him.

He could deal with Jessica; he always talked her down from her crazy better than I ever could.

And Shawn? Well, Shawn was dancing in a tiny skirt.

It wasn't a hard choice.

Well, *it* was hard.

But the choice wasn't.

I pulled her ass against me and started dancing.

She moved in sync with me then stopped and slowly turned in my arms. Her palms went flat against my chest as her face lit up. "You dance?"

"I know, I'm white. It's almost wrong."

She burst out laughing. "I guess I'll just start calling you JT?"

"Or White Usher." I winked.

Finn grabbed her one hand and dragged it south on his chest then stared me down like it was about to get real.

We'd done that before.

Played that game.

Made the crowd go wild.

Eh, why the hell not?

Magic Mike auditions, here we come.

Literally.

Though Finn never advertised it, he was with the stage show during the summer, and I was more than happy to make fun of him every chance I got.

Finn dropped to his knees behind her then twisted his body and pulled her into his arms when I shoved her away and started dancing. Finn ran his hands down her hips as she faced me, while I walked my hands down her front. Her eyes went wide with shock. We were in front and back, a bit indecent, yeah, but making the crowd lose their minds? Absolutely.

Plus, Shawn knew how to move her body. She was on me in seconds while Finn was behind her moving her hips with his hands. I grabbed her left leg, my fingers digging in to her thigh. Her lips parted as I grabbed her other thigh and wrapped them both around my waist as I ground against her. She lay back against Finn as I spread her legs wide and bent down, slowly kissing the inside of her right thigh then her left. Her eyes fluttered closed as her lips parted. People screamed around us. All I saw was her look of ecstasy as I moved my head to her left thigh, a few inches higher, and swirled my tongue against her bare skin. With a bite, I inched higher until I could see bare ass cheek, and I squeezed with my hands in time to the music pulsing through the building.

I pulled her off Finn and into my arms, her legs still wrapped around me as I ground against her again. Then Finn was reaching around me, tugging her to her feet and picking her up, wrapping her legs around him as if we were each getting a turn, when I knew, once this night was over, that mouth was mine.

She let out a little laugh in Finn's arms, like it was fun. But in mine? In mine, she sighed; in mine, I could feel the heaviness of her gaze. He ducked his head toward her neck and kissed down to her collarbone. I clenched my fists and almost yanked her off him and punched him in the dick. He winked at me over her head.

I needed new friends who had no game.

Immediately.

With one more kiss where he made sure to make fucking eye contact with me over her shoulder, he set her on her feet, turned her toward me, and ran his hands in a silhouette fashion down her body until he was on his knees behind her, his hands on her hips. He twisted them, causing her to do a little bit of a salsa-shimmy facing me. I leaned forward and pressed a finger to her chin, then reached around her and dipped her backward. My mouth was on hers before Finn could get braver and push me further. The music ended, people went wild, but all I cared about, all I noticed, was the fact that when the music was gone. She was in my arms, not his.

Her breasts pressed against my chest as I pulled her into my embrace and kissed her harder, tasting the whiskey on her breath and the sweet mint she'd sucked earlier the way I wanted her to suck me.

We broke apart when a new song started. Our eyes locked.

Finn wrapped an arm around each of us. "That was fun."

Shawn clung to me as if she was having trouble using her legs. By the time we made it off the dance floor, women were throwing themselves at Finn like he had the cure for lack of orgasms. He grabbed numbers, bras, and one pair of panties that he threw back into the crowd.

Leo was sipping his drink at the bar, clapping. "Well done. I saw a girl pass out the minute you kissed Shawn's thigh. I think it was death by dancing orgasm. Either that, or she just got too hot."

Shawn grabbed the drink from his hand and downed it.

"That good or that bad?" Leo asked, crossing his arms.

She swayed a bit, pressed her hands to her temples, and swung around so fast I stumbled backward.

Her mouth claimed mine before I could protest.

I was perfectly sober.

Yet she was somehow making me drunk.

Leo and Finn could have burned the place down, and I wouldn't have known. All I knew was that she'd jumped into my arms and hooked her legs around me. I could feel her heat. I could feel every pulse of her blood roaring for more, and I was more than happy to give it to her.

I pulled back just in time to eye Leo. "Make sure her friend makes it home safe…" I made a get over here ASAP with my fingers then grabbed Shawn's hand and drug her out of there.

I had driven my car since I knew I would the sober one.

I all but shoved her inside, buckled her up, and was speeding back to the dorms without even asking if she wanted to go.

Because she made me want to ravish her in the best way possible. Every time we stopped at a light, she ran her fingers along my thigh like she was reliving the dance. I finally just grabbed her hand so she'd stop the torture. Everything was fine. We were about two miles from campus when she started slowly rubbing her thumb across our joined hands.

It was simple.

Tender.

This was not normal hand holding.

I nearly ran through the next stop sign because I glanced at her. I slammed the brakes hard. "Shit." I hit the steering wheel with my free hand. "Sorry, it snuck up on me."

Shawn squeezed my hand harder. "The stop sign? Or the lack of traffic."

I smirked and stared straight ahead. "You'll pay for that."

"What?"

"Act as innocent as you want. I'll enjoy bringing out every single dirty part of you…"

I glanced down as she moved her legs then crossed her ankles like she was squeezing her thighs together.

"Won't help, Shower Girl. Won't help. But you can try."

"What?" Her voice was husky and a little bit raspy.

"Clenching your thighs. Sad replacement. Trust me on this."

"Trust you," she repeated the phrase, and it hung heavy between us.

"Yeah." I kissed her hand and tried like hell not to fly off the side of the road, park, and tug her skirt up.

"How drunk are you?" I asked once we made it back to the dorm. I cut the engine and waited. My breathing had slowed by then, though just barely.

Her eyes pierced straight through me. "One drink, two glasses of water, and a half gulp of whatever Leo was drinking that tasted like orange juice."

I sighed in relief. "Leo rarely drinks. It *was* orange juice with a splash of lime."

"It was good."

"I'll relay the message," I said gruffly before grabbing Shawn and kissing the hell out of her, tasting the orange juice on her tongue and memorizing the way it slid against mine. I pulled away. "Inside. Now."

She opened her door, straight up took off her heels, and jumped onto my back when I came around the front of the car.

I laughed and jogged inside.

People stared.

They could all go to hell.

It took me three tries to get the damn door to our suite open, and when I did, it was to see Slater sleeping on the couch with the remote in his hand.

"We have to sneak by Dad," Shawn whispered against my ear, tickling it then tugging it with her teeth.

I slipped and nearly ran into the countertop. "You can't bite me if you want me to be quiet."

She bit me again.

I held my moan in and tripped over a throw pillow with her still hanging on my back.

Her muffled laughter filled the room as I finally got to

my door and pulled out my keys.

Slater moaned and turned on his side.

I held my breath.

He blinked at the TV then closed his eyes again.

With an exhale, I waited for a loud commercial then slowly opened my door, crossed the threshold, and closed it.

Shawn slid down my back.

I turned the lock.

It was loud.

So loud.

Then silence.

Just our heavy breathing in the dark.

And the fact that at any minute Slater could come running and ruin everything with one truth bomb.

I braced my hands against the door, still not facing her. "Tell me you won't scream."

"Are your hands going to be on me?"

"Yeah."

"Are you going to be touching me?"

"Hell, yeah."

"Then I can't promise I won't scream."

I looked over my shoulder. "At least promise me you'll try to muffle it in the pillow."

"Where's the fun in that?" She winked.

"Fuck, where have you been all my life?"

She peeled her crop top over her head and dropped it to the floor. "Oh, you know, learning how to use a microwave. Electronics are *hard*." She allowed her gaze to sink lower until it fell below my belt.

"Cute." I took a step, then two, and suddenly my hands were on her warm waist, and I was praying I could die between her breasts, or at least let them suffocate me for a good five minutes. "I mean it. Try not to scream. You scream... he comes running... my murder will be on your conscience."

"What a way to die, though." She shrugged.

"Oh? And what position do you think he's going to find us in?"

"The first time or the second?" She backed up.

I chased her and grinned as I brushed a kiss across her mouth. "Innocent little Shower Girl, I meant the fourth."

Chapter Twenty-Nine

Shawn

I WAS TRYING to play it cool when really my heart was pounding way too fast inside my body, and I knew at any time he was going to take one look at me and bail, right? Or say it was all a joke. Or worse, he'd say something stupid like, *"And this is where we're done teaching you all you need to know, young grasshopper. Hurry. Run free. Go make sweet love to another poor college student while we critique your every move."*

A sense of lightheaded giddiness overcame me when he took another step closer.

And then his shirt was being flung to the ground, and his hands moved to the button of his jeans. I held my breath as he very slowly and deliberately unbuttoned then lowered the zipper.

The sound was so loud I could almost feel the vibrations against the air.

If anything would wake up Slater, it would be that stupid zipper. I licked my lips as his abs actually glistened like he'd just casually rubbed coconut oil on all the chunky muscles in preparation for a photo shoot. I reached out, and my hand caressed the third ab down; it was hard and sizzling hot. I pressed my full palm against his skin then slid that same hand down until I was able to shove his hands away.

"Are you going to undress me now?" he smirked.

"I was toying with the idea." I ran my knuckles down the front of his abs again. "But I tend to get distracted by big... thick... bulging... things."

Knox's laugh was seductive, low, but I noticed he was breathing a bit faster. "Well, you're in luck. I have just the thing."

"No way," I teased. "Think I'll be impressed?"

"Some may even say *obsessed*." His lips met mine in a quick peck before he guided both of my hands to his jeans.

I gripped the fabric and tried not to stare too hard as the curve of his ass came into view. I'd never thought guys' asses could be nice. Then again, I'd never seen one that looked like Knox's. Tight in all the right places, smooth. I was almost jealous.

I slid the pants down.

"No boxers or briefs?" I whispered into the night air. "Scandalous."

"I don't like restriction." His half-lidded gaze drank me in. Then his jeans landed on the floor, and something that needed my immediate attention was between us.

"You weren't exaggerating." I gulped, but fascination drove me to explore. Almost breathlessly, I ran my thumb over his tip until his length twitched, and he tensed. Amused, I repeated the move. I bent forward, ready to take him in my mouth, but his hands on my shoulders prevented me from tasting. For now.

His mouth crashed against mine as he picked me up in his arms and flung us both onto his bed. We landed with his weight on his elbows.

I met his kiss, deepening it, giving him my tongue, my mouth, pressing my body so tight against him that I could feel his heat pulsing against my thigh, while I too pulsed in intimate places. He was right; clenching my thighs didn't help — not when my body was demanding he fill it hard and fast. Who was I kidding? I'd wanted him the minute I saw him then I'd fallen hard when he'd opened his mouth and even harder each day after, until it was impossible to say anything but yes.

He moved on top of me, shifting slightly as his hand inched up my skirt, his eyes never losing focus while he watched me watching him. Mouth suddenly dry, I waited for him to say something to break the tension, something to get me out of my head. Wasn't that what these guys did?

His hand came into contact with my bare butt cheek. He squeezed and gave his head a shake. "I thought you were wearing a thong when we were dancing, and the whole time I could have just bent you over the bar and had my way with you?"

"And risked possible jail time, yes," I answered with a breathy sigh that made me feel equal parts aroused and stupid. I wasn't that girl, the one who just randomly slept with guys who looked like movie stars, but it was Knox.

And even if I wasn't his game changer…

He felt like mine.

He squeezed, his head descended, and his hot mouth pressed an open kiss to my neck as he tugged my skirt down my legs. I was completely exposed to him, his skin so steamy against mine. Yet I shivered. I wanted to feel more of him, more of our bodies sliding against each other, his hard against my soft.

"Remember..." He nuzzled my neck, his words hot against my ear. "...no screaming equals no death."

"No death."

With his lips, he tugged my earlobe.

A shiver rippled through me, even though my body burned and throbbed with need. "Yeah, got it, no... death."

Knox let out a dark chuckle against my neck then pulled back, his eyes searching mine. "I haven't done this in three years."

"I haven't done this... ever."

His eyes went so wide, his skin so pale, that I nearly died laughing. "I'm joking! You should have seen your face!"

"Oh, you think that's funny?" He reached for my hips and pulled me first to a sitting position then over his shoulder until my bare ass was facing the ceiling. And next, he slapped — hard enough to make it sting, hard enough to make my thighs clench together with each hit. Then it started feeling different... good. Pain moved toward pleasure at such an alarming rate that I let out a moan.

Each stinging slap drove a spike of tingling desire directly to my core. The muscles at my center clenched and unclenched as my most intimate place literally wept for him to fill me.

Crack. This time his palm lingered, and his fingers that were clenched around my ass cheek squeezed firmly before sliding off. I gasped as air hit the spot he'd vacated, and then...

Crack. His palm slid across stinging skin, and he grazed

the sensitive spot between my legs with his fingertips. I writhed beneath his touch, wanting more…

Oh, so much more.

What was he doing to me?

Crack. I bit down on my lip to keep from screaming then his hand was at my mouth, gently covering. I bit down on his fingers lightly. That slap had been harder, but the memory of his fingers brushing against my core at the same time made me tremble as the fiery, throbbing need built.

His hand left my mouth as I let out a gasp.

Crack. One finger breached my most intimate place and stayed inside. Groaning, I clenched my muscles around that finger. My body shook as I tried to hold on. "More," I ordered. "More."

With a sharp intake of breath, he pulled back and slapped me once more. I rocked against him, the tips of my breasts rubbing against his naked back, the motion making my nipples ache to have his mouth there.

"Damn, they feel good everywhere, don't they?" he murmured, rubbing my ass with his right hand then pulling me down so I straddled his lap. His mouth was on mine before I could answer.

My body tingled and shook with awareness. So close… I just had to move a few inches… He rubbed against me, driving me crazy. He was all velvet heat, and I was more than ready to invite him in.

He kissed me harder, deeper. I was lost in his taste, in the way his hair felt wrapped around my fingers as I moved on top of him. His hands left my back as the sound of a condom wrapper tearing filled the air. There wasn't any fumbling, no laughing, just desperation on both our parts as he broke away from me. I licked my lips in anticipation.

A click then total silence came from the main room. The TV had been turned off.

"Hey…" A knock sounded on the door. "…you guys back yet?"

Knox's chest heaved as he slowly shook his head at me.

I nodded and grabbed the condom. I unrolled it and slowly sheathed him.

He gritted his teeth as I moved my hand up and down lightly and winked.

"Guys?" Slater called again.

Knox bit down on his lip so hard it turned white.

With one fluid movement, he gripped me by the hips and slid me down onto him. There had been no warning, only complete fullness that had me opening my mouth on a scream.

He clapped a hand over my mouth and moved.

I felt my eyes roll back as my body responded. I gripped his shoulders while Slater stood on the other side of the door.

"Guys?" He knocked again.

Knox moved faster then pulled out and jerked me into his arms. He walked me backward toward the very door where Slater was, no doubt, still standing. My eyes must have been wide because he smirked like it was the funniest thing he'd ever seen, and when he pressed my bare ass against the wood and entered me, shoving me harder against the door, I almost kicked him. My lips parted again. I'd never had to be quiet before. I didn't think I could now.

But this time I had no choice.

And it felt so good I wanted the world to know that it was Knox doing this, only Knox.

My legs shook as pleasure built between us, nearly combusting when Knox kissed down my neck only to come back to my mouth and swallow my next whimper as if he knew I'd been about to lose it.

And when the sound of footsteps retreating filled the empty space behind the door, I breathed a sigh of relief. Knox clenched his teeth. I was so close, yet impressed that it had been three years, but the guy had the stamina of a rock star.

"Remember," he panted, "no screams."

"And…" I moaned as he went deeper, making my vision momentarily blur as my body tightened then gave and adjusted to him. "…if I have to?"

"Death." He chuckled and slowed his thrusts, driving me crazy. I pounded my fist against his chest.

"You're stopping why?"

"Eh, just building up your climax, Shower Girl." He winked. "Lean back."

"What?"

He sat me on the desk and pushed me back. "Over the desk, lean backward at an angle."

Then I lost all consciousness, or it felt like it, when our bodies slid together, and with his fingers, he thoroughly explored unknown territory, according to my last ex-boyfriend, whose idea of sex was two minutes long and a nice high-five afterward.

"Knox—" I clamped my teeth together. "—I—"

He slammed his mouth against mine, and I greedily took all I could get, ripping at his hair and pulling him hard against me as wave after wave rocked through my core like a category-12 tsunami. My legs turned to complete jelly when he followed and whispered with a dark promise, "Round one, position two… give me forty minutes. Oh, and Shower Girl? Better hydrate."

Chapter Thirty

Knox

"Does this mean I get to cut your hair now?" Shawn murmured sleepily.

My body was tight in all the right places. My muscles ached, and all I wanted was a nice massage and a few more rounds before Slater murdered me for screwing his roommate.

I knew exactly how that conversation would go.

Which meant we couldn't tell him.

Not if I wanted to stay alive.

And not if I wanted to keep my past in the past.

"I might make you work for it a bit more," I teased, running my hands through her thick hair, giving it a tug and examining how it glistened against her warm mocha skin. Touching her was necessary; my fingers itched with the need to caress every damn time I saw her.

And I would never tell her the effect she had on me.

Because it would put the ball in her court. She'd be the favorite to win whatever game this was, and the last time I gave it all…

I'd lost it all.

"You all right?" Shawn turned on her side and faced me, her eyes searching mine. "Or are you just trying to find a polite way to send me back to my room?"

I frowned. "You do realize we have about five minutes before the guys come barging in here, right?"

Her smile fell.

I wrapped my arms around her tighter. "Stay the night."

"Pretty sure my mom warned me about threesomes…"

I tilted my head. "Wow, progressive mom."

She blushed. "Okay, maybe not my mom, but you know, books, society, humans— Sharing isn't caring, at least not in my book."

"Look at me." I gripped her chin and gazed deep into her eyes. "I wouldn't share you with them if they were both being held at gunpoint."

"Wow!" Finn swept into the room. "Good to know, bro."

Leo just shook his head. "And to think, I put you in my will."

I rolled on to my back and clenched my teeth. "You're early."

"Yeah, well, Finn drove as slowly as he physically could. A cop even pulled us over because we looked suspicious in that brand new Jeep. I almost told her she had a nice ass then decided you'd be pissed if you had to bail us both out of jail, so we got by with a warning, and I took a mental picture for later."

Finn nodded, obviously lost in thought. "See? You noticed her ass. I'll raise you two gorgeous blue eyes."

Leo squinted. "Touché."

"Turn around." I pointed. "Both of you."

"We've seen you naked." Leo shrugged.

"But you haven't seen Shawn—" I growled when Leo smirked. "Say what's on your mind, and I'm going to throw you out the window. We have a rosebush two floors down, so think carefully."

Leo eyed me with humor then finally lifted his hands into the air and turned around. Finn did the same.

I quickly jumped out of bed, grabbed a pair of sweats and a shirt, and tossed them to Shawn.

Her cheeks were flushed a deep crimson as she pulled on the pants, jerking them over her hips without getting out from under the sheets. She pulled the shirt over her head, catching some of that beautiful hair before pulling it out and flashing me an easy grin. Like this was normal.

As if changing in a guy's room with two other guys was just how she rolled on a daily basis after having sex.

After being with me.

I was completely out of my element.

Because this was the part where I sucked.

The part where I'd forgotten how to be normal.

I knew how to please women after they'd been discarded, tossed aside, and told they were worthless.

What I didn't know how to do?

Talk to the woman who already knew her worth and saw it reflected in my eyes.

How the fuck was I going to keep her?

How was I going to stay sane?

And how was I going to make sure she didn't see the ugly part of my past? I wasn't stupid. I knew she needed my trust.

And no woman in her right mind would trust me.

They had reasons not to.

Ones I was sure Slater would be more than happy to list then laminate so Shawn wouldn't forget.

I ran my hands through my hair. "You guys can turn back around now."

"We were just talking about cutting Knox's hair." Shawn pulled her knees to her chest. "Weren't we?"

"Uh, pretty sure it was barely on the table for discussion." I chuckled and sat back down on my bed.

The room smelled like sweat, like sex, like us. I inhaled deeply then leaned in and kissed her neck. She shivered under my touch.

"You know…" Finn sighed. "…it's not often that I'm left out of scenarios like this. I'm not sure I like it."

"I fucking hate it," Leo piped up. "I feel like I walked into a candy store, and the dickless manager just told me it was closed."

"You're the dickless manager," Finn said, grabbing a pair of scissors from the desk and pointing them at me.

"Got that, thanks." I rolled my eyes.

"Just one taste." Leo sauntered over.

I stood and clenched my fists.

He slow-clapped. "That's how you know—"

"You love her!" Finn joined in on the singing.

"Hey, I love that movie!" Shawn fell back against the pillows and laughed. "That's how you know you're the one!"

"Unbelievable," I muttered. "It's like I found the one girl who understands how to deal with you two."

"It's a beautiful thing." Leo shoved me out of the way then sat on the bed, pulled Shawn's feet onto his lap, and started massaging. "So, I hope he was tender with you."

"Leo!" I roared.

Finn nodded then moved behind her and started massaging her shoulders. "I mean, when it's been three years, sometimes a little…" They both turned to glare at me. "…enthusiasm can be a bad thing."

I covered my face with my hands and wished a swift death on both my best friends just as a knock sounded at the door.

"Guys?" It was Slater.

I took in Shawn's mussed hair and swollen lips, plus the fact that she looked like I'd just fucked her into the weekend.

"I got this," Leo whispered and twisted her foot a bit, pressed down first on the middle of it then on her big toe, and suddenly she was shivering as if she was cold.

"Good, Leo! Make her tits show through her shirt more!" I hissed.

"Sorry!" Leo looked and looked again. "Sorry again? I panicked!"

"Wrong pressure point, genius." Finn sighed then ran over, lit a candle, pulled off his shirt, and rubbed coconut oil down his chest. He did a few jumping jacks and opened the door. "Hey there, sailor."

Slater backed up, hands raised.

"Oh." Finn sighed. "Sorry, thought it was Rory. He just got dumped again, wanted to do a little bit of role-playing. You know how he likes the ocean." Finn flashed him the biggest shit-eating grin I'd ever seen.

Slater just shook his head as if he was thanking God he still didn't work for Wingman, Inc. then looked past Finn. "Shawn?"

"Hey! We were just going to watch a movie? Wanna hang?"

"No." Slater sighed. "I don't want to *hang*." He made

air quotes then stared me down. "Thought we talked about this."

"She was with me, dipshit," Leo piped up. "And she wanted to go out dancing with Alexa. I thought it would be smarter for her to take a sober-buddy than go by herself and get into trouble."

Slater paled. "Uh, yeah, good point."

They were both covering for me.

"Plus, the big guy's sick." Leo nodded to me.

I coughed. It was weak.

But Slater must have bought it because he visibly relaxed.

"I was just trying to be s-safe." Shawn choked on the word, her gaze wide as I turned to her.

Finn's eyes narrowed while Slater came closer.

Then Finn looked to the right, by the chair, and grinned so big I wanted to punch him in the teeth. He leaned down as if he was grabbing something off the floor and picked up a condom wrapper. He mouthed, *"One?"* then grinned. *"Two?"* He coughed. *"Three?"*

I would be murdered tonight.

"Safety…" Finn shoved them in his pocket. "…is extremely important. You never know when you might catch something. I mean, take diseases, STDs—"

So killing him. I am going to put a pillow over his face and hold it there until his legs stop flopping.

"—can be scary as shit," he finished.

"Right." Slater was looking at Shawn, though, not at any of us. Then he leaned down and grabbed her hands. "Why didn't you call me?"

"You've been busy. Plus, I thought you were still gone."

"I came back early." He sighed. "And you know I'd cancel anything for you."

Jealousy reared its ugly head. I clenched my fists.

Finn shook his head no while Leo mouthed at me to calm the hell down.

My body felt hot and wild, like I was ready for Slater to challenge me, to call me out. Hell, I was more than ready to run my fist through his face.

He was touching her.

It was different when it was Leo and Finn. Although their actions had sometimes irritated me, I knew they were innocent. I knew they didn't date, other than one-night stands. Besides, they'd pushed me into this. And we didn't share with each other, not that way.

"I know." Shawn cupped his face. "I'm a big girl though, 'kay? I figured it out."

Hell yeah, she did.

Three times she'd figured it out. Dipshit.

Slater exhaled and stood. "Fine, so what are we watching?"

"Eyes Wide Shut," Leo said loud and clear. "It's Finn's favorite."

Bullshit! Finn hadn't even seen it.

Great, I was going to watch all the sex and all the orgies…

An hour after being with Shawn.

An hour after needing to be inside her again.

An hour after trying to decide how I was going to keep her by my side when I knew it was better for her to be across the living room.

"Well?" Slater shrugged. "We doing this?"

"Yup." Finn started walking out of the room. "Oh, and Slater?"

"What?"

"I've missed your winning personality."

"Bite me."

"See?" He winked. "He's ba-a-ack."

Chapter Thirty-One

Shawn

Those movies? Where you had four hot guys surrounding you, and each and every one of them knew what you needed before you even said it out loud?

That didn't exist in real life.

Because it's not real.

Yet there I was, sitting with Slater in front of me warming up my legs and feet.

Finn to the right, handing me popcorn before I could reach for the bowl.

Leo to the left, providing the straw I hadn't asked for, to the soda I hadn't even known he'd held until he lifted it to my lips and winked, because clearly, I looked parched. Then there was Knox.

Directly behind me.

Arms crossed.

Sitting in a chair, huffing out his frustration every few

minutes, and somehow, I noticed him the most.

Maybe it was his body heat.

Maybe it was the raw hunger I could feel penetrating the walls around my body. Or maybe it was just the fact that every few seconds, his hands were in my hair as if he couldn't stay away.

Maybe he had no choice but to touch me.

This right here was *not* what I'd signed up for when I decided to transfer schools, yet, I couldn't pinpoint why it didn't feel wrong. Was it because I trusted them?

Leo joked, but I also knew there was this line he'd drawn that he knew not to cross. Finn was all kinds of charismatic, but he truly put others before himself. It was obvious that Slater was protective and concerned about my intense practice schedule.

I knew Knox and I— What we had felt different.

It didn't feel like any of my other relationships.

I just wished I could have had that normal girl freak-out moment after sex where you called your best friend and gushed about all the things then asked if you were being ridiculous for picking out your wedding dress.

I sighed.

I wasn't exactly shopping for shoes yet.

And I wasn't sure if Alexa and I were close enough to even talk about that sort of thing. If I was being really honest? My insecurity was rearing its ugly head in a choking way.

"My parents just… they don't understand." Jack ran *his hands over his face and groaned in irritation. "But they're paying for school, you know?"*

My blood ran cold. "No, maybe you should just spell it out for me, since last night you were telling me you loved me, and right now it sounds like you're dumping me!" I started to shake uncontrollably. No. It couldn't be happening. Not again. I had promised myself this time I'd be careful.

Keep my heart close.

Especially when dating a white guy who drove a shiny brand new BMW and had a daddy who was from the South.

The warning signs were there with his background. But who was I to judge? And he'd promised.

He'd promised!

Jack bit down on his bottom lip and reached out for me. It was exactly what I needed.

I walked into his arms and laid my head on his shoulder. "I hate this."

Tears filled my eyes. "Me too."

"But…"

There it was.

I tensed.

He pulled back. "Shawn, I love you. I do. You're gorgeous, talented. Hell, any guy on campus would do anything to be with you."

He was right about one thing. They wanted to be with me.

Keeping me was something else altogether.

Being seen with me?

My parents warned me that not every place was as progressive as New York. I hadn't listened.

Not until going to LSU.

"Look." Jack's smile was forced; he was all white teeth and old money, with a housekeeper who had the same color skin as I, and a gardener who had such a thick Southern accent I couldn't understand a word he said. "It will blow over. Just give it time." He squeezed my hand. "I mean, I'll talk to Dad, but he sort of holds all the cards in his hands right now."

"So, that's it." Anger surged through me. "You're dumping me because your dad's a racist pig!"

Tears streamed down my face.

Jack released me as anger flashed so quickly I almost missed it. "What the hell do you know?" he sneered. "He's my father. I know you're not used to this sort of lifestyle, but that's just how things are done! If I'm supposed to take over the firm, I need to follow the rules. Then once I prove myself, I'll choose whoever I want by my side, and I want you."

"Romantic," I said through clenched teeth as I crossed my arms.

He didn't say anything.

I mean, what was there left to say?

"Goodbye, Jack," I whispered, wiping away the tears of betrayal and hurt. Wiping away the dreams of a big, fancy wedding and the pretty engagement ring I had seen on my finger the minute he'd said, "I love you."

What if history repeated itself?

If Knox hadn't wanted me to keep him forever, he shouldn't have given me a taste of what a few minutes in his arms would feel like. A girl could get used to those minutes and wonder what would happen if there were more minutes on top of the other minutes.

I tensed.

Maybe it was just a one-time thing.

I could do that.

I could be okay with that.

I just needed to not get any more attached to his perfect smile or the way that, whenever I looked into his eyes, I didn't see judgement, just a bit of obsession, which made me want him even more.

"Gummy worm?" Finn shoved one in my mouth.

I sucked it between my lips and chewed.

"Where did that even come from?"

"His sweaty pocket," Knox growled behind me.

Finn ignored him while Leo held the straw to my mouth and winked. "Sip?"

"I'm not a child. I can hold my own can of soda."

"Ri-i-ght," Leo said slowly like he was trying to figure me out. "But you're relaxing. I have two hands, so why would you when I can do it for you?"

I opened my mouth to argue when Slater grunted out, "Wingman Fantasy Frat Rule Number Two."

"Huh?" I repeated while Knox went, "Shhhh."

"Wingman Fantasy Frat? That's what you are?"

"Technically." Slater put up air quotes. "At least, that's how they get paid, right?"

"Are you billing me right now?" I was ready to shoot up from my chair and rage around the living room.

Leo sighed. "Mood wrecker."

Finn threw popcorn at Slater's head while Knox put his hands on my shoulders.

I instantly relaxed.

"We don't bill our friends, asshole," was Knox's terse response to Slater. "Let them do something nice for her because they're genuinely nice guys, not that you would know, since you cut us out three years ago, but—"

The room fell silent.

The buzz of the TV was the only sound I could hear above my own heavy breathing as tension wrapped around us all like a knife.

"Yeah? Well, when you're questioned by the police and someone dies, things tend to get a bit depressing. Right, Knox? Or is that not the word you would use?"

"No shit-talking during movie-night," Finn said in a tight voice, flashing me one of his smiles while Leo looked down at his lap, put the soda in one hand then grabbed my hand and squeezed.

At first, I thought it was because he was trying to reassure me.

Then I realized it.

The way he looked at me.

The way he tensed in his seat.

He wanted me to reassure him.

So I did. I squeezed his hand back and smiled.

He nodded then jerked his head back toward Knox, who had gone completely silent behind us.

Until the door to the suite slammed.

"Where'd he go?" I asked the room.

Nobody answered.

I moved to get up, but Slater held my legs tight. "Let him go."

"But—"

"I said let him fucking go." Slater turned up the volume.

I held Leo's hand the rest of the movie.

And when Finn noticed, *he* wrapped an arm around me, and they kept me close.

I'd often wondered what it would be like to have crazy protective big brothers. I suddenly knew — only it hurt to look at all of them at the same time. They were protective,

they were fierce.
They were mine.

Chapter Thirty-Two

Knox

"Hey," I said dumbly when Shawn ran back in to the suite after what appeared to be a grueling practice. It had been less than twelve hours since I was inside her, since I'd tasted her, felt her body tighten in all the right places. Damn it, I wanted more. And all I had was a *"hey"*?

"Hey, yourself." She was a bit out of breath.

Exhaustion looked good on her. Damn good. It would only look better if a workout with me had been the thing that had exhausted her. Her cheeks went pink as if she knew that I'd suddenly thought up a list of every single pink thing on her that I wanted to lick.

"I have to teach Human Anatomy today. Want me to give you a ride?" That sounded good, not desperate. I just wanted to be next to her, even if it meant I couldn't be kissing her skin. I'd just seen Slater take off, so it would be an easy way for us to talk.

Because if I knew anything about women, it was that they had to talk after sex.

And no chance in hell was I letting that talk be with any of the males currently at her beck and call.

Fuck no. If she wanted to talk about sex between us...

It was me.

Or the wall.

"You look upset." She tilted her head then held up her finger, ran into her room, and came back a few seconds later with her messenger bag, a cute red beanie that she shoved over her pretty hair, and a bottle of water. She held up her hand again, dashed out of the room and returned with another bottle and tossed it to me.

"I'm not upset." I smiled and unscrewed the water. "And thanks."

"Glad you're not upset, and even more thankful for the ride. I was about to be five minutes late, and the last thing I need—" She pulled her hair over her shoulder while I took a long sip of water. "—is for the TA to spank me over his desk because I'm not on time."

I choked on a mouthful of water, nearly spewing it out into the air.

She winked.

"Shit." My hoarse voice came out louder than I thought. "You realize all I'm going to be thinking about is spanking you, right? For an entire damn hour?"

"Oh, I'm counting on it." She eyed me up and down then focused her attention right where I wanted it.

I'd never gotten so hard so fast in my entire life, and I was wearing the tightest damn jeans on the planet.

"Thinking about it now?"

"I have a very vivid imagination." I put my hand on

the small of her back while I carefully adjusted myself then walked her down the hall and out of the building. "In fact, I'm imagining your naked body spread out on that very same desk with your legs wide open just begging me to take you."

She stumbled on flat ground.

I caught her elbow and whispered, "Two can play that game."

"Yeah, but can we both win?" She tapped her chin with her finger.

"As long as I'm inside you, and you're screaming my name, I think that's what they call teamwork and winning, don't you?"

She licked her lips as her eyes drank me in like the only thing she wanted to do was me.

Forever.

God, I'd missed that feeling.

The feeling of being wanted.

The electric pulses of magnetic lust that pounded around two individuals whose hearts raced too fast. I could almost hear her heart taking flight while blood pinked her cheeks… and other places I desperately wanted to kiss.

Later.

After class.

I sighed and looked up. "It's going to be the longest day of my life, isn't it?"

"I have a two-hour break after Human Anatomy." She shrugged a shoulder while I opened her door and helped her in, and because I lacked all sorts of self-control, I kissed her.

Softly.

Not because I was getting paid.

Not because she had a broken heart.

But because I'd wanted to.

And it was the first time in years I'd done something selfishly.

I loved it.

Needed it.

My heart sped up a bit as she licked my lower lip. How she got her mouth so damn soft I'd never know.

"What was that for?" she asked in a voice I knew all too well. It was breathless; it was wanting confirmation; it said and asked all the things I knew we needed to discuss in one simple question. It was also the first time I'd seen uncertainty flicker across her face. I hated it. I hated even more that the reason for it had to do with my employment with Wingman, Inc. and my reputation around campus.

"A kiss," I said after a few seconds of searching her deep brown eyes. "A damn good kiss."

She pressed her palm to my cheek and leaned in. "I've had better."

"Liar." I walked around the car, got in, andstarted the engine.

She laughed, making me smile all the more as we drove around campus and finally found a parking spot.

I killed the engine, got out, and walked over to her side. She was already opening her door.

"Let me be a gentleman at least once in my life," I murmured, helping her out of the car then dropping her hand.

Campus was busy. Students were everywhere, and one by one, as per usual, the whisperings began, the staring continued, and I could feel every single pair of eyes on the back of my heated neck.

Normally, I'd have put on my sunglasses and ignored everyone, pretending I was better than each human being surrounding me.

But today I didn't feel normal.

My armor wasn't in place.

My pissed-off demeanor had been completely calmed by the gorgeous woman standing next to me, leaving me vulnerable, drained, out of control, and stuck in a bit of a sexual chaos that my body was still trying to cool down from.

"So…" Shawn grabbed my hand and squeezed it.

Then didn't let go.

I stared down at our joined hands like she'd just announced she was from ET's planet and needed my touch to stay alive.

I mean.

We were holding hands.

Fucking. Hands.

I didn't hold hands.

Not with women.

Not on campus.

Not since… her.

People knew that about me.

It was like the sad story you pass down to freshman to warn them away from parties, drugs, and guys with easy smiles and too much money.

I was the warning story.

It was why it made sense to stick with Wingman, Inc.

I could play the part for their own sick entertainment, while at the same time, making money and earning out my internship hours.

But now? Now that Shawn was holding my hand, it was like I suddenly felt even more empty than before.

More terrified.

Of the moment she found out, dropped my hand, and

walked out of my life like she should.

"You're holding my hand," I blurted, squeezing her fingers back as we headed toward the science building.

"Yeah, you looked a bit panicked."

"I don't panic," I said quickly.

"Sure you don't." Her voice was calm, her teasing tone gone, almost like she knew that I was having a mental breakdown and needed support.

What the hell was wrong with me?

Here I was getting ready to have the talk with her, and I couldn't even get past the fact that we were holding hands and walking into the building together.

Down the hall.

More whispers.

Shit, this was a bad idea.

I didn't let go, though.

Once we got to the classroom she let go of my hand and made her way up to Leo.

His eyebrows were basically caught up in his beanie as his jaw dropped to his desk. He held out a coffee to her while slurping on his own Frappuccino. His shit-eating grin was the last thing I needed right now.

As more students filtered in…

My anxiety dissipated.

And anger quickly took its place.

Anger at myself.

Anger at the students around us who were most likely tweeting about the hand-holding and saying nasty things about a girl they, no doubt, assumed had paid for the favor.

Fuck.

That was where my sexual hiatus left me.

With the one girl who didn't pay me for it.

And an entire campus who thought she did.

Chapter Thirty-Three

Shawn

MY NECK HEATED as notifications started going off on my phone. Twitter and Instagram pictures with me tagged in them, and some with a giant question mark over my head. As if they were confused.

That made two of us.

Another tweet came through.

> Forget tasting the rainbow. @KnoxT just wants a bit of chocolate milk. Too bad she's a client.

The next one was worse.

> Wonder how much @SoftballShawn paid him to hold her hand. Anyone else having flashbacks from 3 yrs ago?

Three years ago? What the heck happened three years ago?

My phone buzzed again. Leo swiped it from the desk and slid it into his pocket then wrapped a protective arm around me and whispered, "It's just campus gossip. They're bored. Don't take it to heart."

"Kinda hard not to."

He squeezed.

Knox's eyes roamed the room before finally locking on mine.

I'd never quite understood the whole dream people always said they had on the first day school where they imagined themselves standing in front of everyone naked. At least, not until that point. Now, I felt exposed, watched, judged. I felt myself being weighed and found wanting.

I felt my eyes burning with unshed tears as I thought back to my last university and the guy I'd left there after being told that he loved me — but not enough to stand up for me to his own father.

My skin… it was a problem.

"White boys don't marry mixed black girls."

His dad's exact words.

Oh, I was good enough to date, but marry? No. It was just a phase. Get the wild out of your system and all that.

His words had stung so badly that night when I'd heard their hushed conversation and when Jack said nothing then ended the conversation with, *"I understand, sir."*

Only to dump me the next day.

The emotional knife had sliced deep.

I had run away from the pain to start new, but somehow that pain was finding its way back into my consciousness. It wasn't my fault. No, this was their problem. Why did it always have to be about race?

If they saw my heart, it beat the same.

I still bled.

I still wanted.

A tear slid down my cheek.

Leo reached out and snatched it away with his free hand and cursed under his breath as Knox slowly walked around the desk and made his way up the stairs to where I was sitting.

The room quieted.

A muscle in his jaw tensed as he finally gripped the table in front of me with both hands, leaned down, and kissed me soundly on the mouth.

I sighed when the comfort of his hands cupped my face with such tenderness another tear squeezed out before I could stop it.

He pulled away. "Are you okay?"

"I am now," I whispered.

He leaned back, cleared his throat. "Girlfriend. Any questions?"

Everyone was silent.

"Great, since that's cleared up, open your books to Chapter Five…"

And that was it.

The girls in the room had wide eyes and shocked expressions.

And the guys? They didn't even seem fazed.

Nobody was staring anymore.

Well, nobody worth mentioning. Jessica's stare bored into me from across the room.

Her eyes zeroed in with such hate that I almost slid down my chair in an effort to hide. What was wrong with her?

She finally snapped her attention away and raised her

hand to answer a question. Knox refused to call on her, which probably just pissed her off more.

"Ignore her," Leo whispered. "Every once in a while, we get the obsessed crazies. Just chalk her up to one of them. She's been in love with him ever since starting with us three years ago."

"Three years." I gulped. "I think it's about time I ask what happened three years ago that has this entire campus losing their minds, her included."

We were supposed to be reading.

Leo cleared his throat and shook his head just as a shadow cast over our table.

Knox leaned over and said, "Do I need to separate you two?"

"Couldn't if you tried," Leo smirked.

Knox just rolled his eyes. "I was afraid you'd say that." He reached out and touched my shoulder. "Wait for me after class."

Then he made his way back to his desk.

"Teacher's pet," Leo hissed under his breath.

I kicked him.

"Think he'll spank you later?" He grinned. I rolled my eyes as he leaned in and whispered, "Think he'll let me watch?"

I kicked him again, and he burst out laughing then started coughing to cover up his laugh.

"You know, Leo, I can't wait for the day some unsuspecting girl slaps your ass and makes you beg."

He groaned. "I love it when they beg. From your mouth to God's ears, Shower Girl."

"You're impossible."

He put his hand over his heart. "Thank you."

Chapter Thirty-Four

Knox

It was the longest class I'd ever taught in my entire life.

A sharp ache was banging between my ears as I finally dismissed class and waited for everyone to trickle out.

Naturally, Jessica just had to be one of the last ones. I hadn't given her any of my attention, any of my time.

"Knox?" The way she said my name had my skin crawling. What the hell had I been thinking kissing her just to shove the girl I really wanted away? I shuddered at the memory of her touch and glanced up.

"What?" I hadn't meant for it to sound like a bark, but it had come out aggressive and a whole lot of pissed-off.

She took a step back, her face blank before a forced smile appeared. "So, I'm hosting a party this weekend, just a few friends. Do you think you'd like to come and—"

"No," I cut her short. "I'm good. Thanks for the invite."

"But—"

I sighed and dropped the papers from my hands. I slammed my palms against the table. "Leo, take care of this."

I knew he was hanging back with Shawn, so I was killing two birds with one stone.

Leo took the stairs two at a time, but not fast enough to keep Jessica from losing her shit and saying, "Her? Out of all the girls you've been with, me included, you choose a girl who probably doesn't even know who her daddy is? Come on, Knox, you're better than that!"

"Enough!" I roared. Blood pumped through my veins, making my fists clench and unclench. Never had I wanted to hit a woman so badly in my entire life. I breathed in and out at her wide-eyed expression. "Say one more word, and I'll cheerfully ruin your reputation. We keep records of everything, and I'd rather take you down with me and end Wingman, Inc.'s presence on this campus than hear one more word from your bitchy mouth."

She paled.

She had reasons to.

She was one of the clients who'd asked for a little extra, a client who'd often used her time with us to confess all the horrible things she'd done to girls in competition with her. She'd bragged, and we'd recorded everything for safety reasons. Granted, we were never supposed to expose secrets — it was part of our jobs — but I'd rather be tangled in a lawsuit with the bitch than have to deal with one more word from her nasty mouth.

"Fine." She licked her lips, and her eyes flickered to Leo as he casually wrapped an arm around her and led her to the door.

"I ever tell you that time I was in bed for three days?" He laughed, the door clicking shut behind him.

And then there was Shawn.

Beautiful. Sexy. Shawn.

With her messenger bag over one shoulder, her beanie hung low over her eyes, and her hair spread out across her shoulders like a fluffy velvet blanket. It was hard to look away from her gaze, as if she held some sort of power over me that was inexplicable.

"Listen, Shawn, I'm so—"

"Stop." She dropped her messenger bag, walked slowly to the door.

I hung my head.

She pulled the blinds and locked the door then turned.

I waited for her to cry, to tell me it was my fault, that she hated the attention, that I wasn't worth it.

I hadn't expected her to come back.

But she did.

She walked back to me and grabbed the front of my shirt, jerking me toward her. Our bodies crushed together as her mouth met mine in a soulful kiss that said way more than I could with words.

"Thank you," she breathed between peppered kisses and sliding tongues, between hurried hands and the rustle of strained clothing between us. "Thank you," she said again as the line blurred more between right and wrong, secrets and lies.

And I let it blur until all I saw was us as I gripped her by the ass and set her on the desk, as I wrapped her muscled legs around my body and jerked the beanie off her head. I tossed it into the air in an effort to grip her hair without any sort of obstruction.

"I'm not good at this." I stopped what would have been another kiss in a series of hundreds of kisses that would have led to sex on the desk of the professor she hated. In a class she wasn't passing. In a world that wasn't fair. In a time when it should have been.

She beamed, still clinging to the front of my shirt. "I think you're great at this…"

"You know what I mean," I whispered. "I'm not good at the after, the part where the guy tells you he's good, that he won't walk away. I'm not the hero, Shawn."

"Yeah? Well, take it from me. Heroes are disappointing and oftentimes weaker than the villains." She shrugged. "Give me the villain ready to flip off the entire world in an effort to prove a point any day. Give me the guy willing to take down the world for what he believes in. I want that guy."

"It was wrong. It *is* wrong. The way you're treated for being with me." There. I'd said it. The elephant had appeared, and the room tensed again. But her eyes never once left mine as she brought her mouth closer until I could taste her, until my body pulsed with the need to do it again, until she was all I could taste.

"Knox…" Her voice wavered. "…I know what it's like to be treated unfairly." She licked her lips and let the words float into the air, let me absorb them as I took in her brown skin and jet-black hair. "You ignore it the best you can and prove them wrong the only way a fighter knows how."

I sighed. "That's the fucking problem, Shawn."

"What?" Her eyes searched mine.

I wanted to close her off, to keep the truth locked down just a little while longer. "You're innocent," I breathed out. "I'm not."

She sighed.

I expected her to press me further.

Most girls would.

Instead, she just kissed me again, as if it would solve all my problems, all of our problems. And in that second, I forced myself to believe it would. I convinced myself that as long as I had her, I could ignore the demons I hadn't yet dealt with. I could ignore what was causing my gut to clench every single time I saw the look in her eyes.

The look of trust I didn't deserve.

With a moan, I deepened the kiss, desperate to forget, to lose myself in her. I was suddenly thankful she'd decided on wearing joggers as I first pulled off her shoes, next her pants, and kissed her backward toward the locked door, the closed blinds, with the sounds of students laughing and talking just a few feet away from us.

I pressed her back against the door. "Shhhh."

"Are we really doing this. Another door?" Her voice had a bit of thrill in it as she reached for the button of my jeans.

I rubbed myself against her and kissed the crook of her neck then moved her hair aside and nuzzled lower.

"That must be my answer."

"Or this…" I shrugged my jeans down my hips and teased her entrance. Damn, she was so wet and ready for me.

She sighed into my mouth, "Good answer."

"The best." I reached into my pocket to pull out a condom.

"Pill." She kissed me hard enough that I had to grab her to keep from stumbling backward. She used the angle to slide along my length like I was a fucking ride at the fair. Her inner heat seared me then she clamped down with her muscles down there, driving me wild with need.

I liked it.

I liked it too much.

With a moan, I felt my balls tighten as the world stood still, and I became aware that it suddenly wasn't about sex to me.

Maybe it never had been.

It was about her.

I thrust forward in anticipation. She opened to me, accepted me, trusted me. It was beautiful.

It was something I'd never had with another soul.

Her eyes closed as I moved.

My heart soared as she mouthed my name.

Fingers toyed with my shirt as our mouths met, our bodies moving in a slow cadence while the world didn't even know what was happening, or what to listen for. I felt the shift in the universe and knew this was different. She was different.

The ending would not be the same.

A heavy silence descended between us as I pressed feather-light kisses to her jaw, the sweet taste of her skin driving me to the edge as we both spiraled out of control. She writhed against me as I sank deeper into her, my thrusts coming faster and faster. A fury of pleasure hung between us, and my pace quickened. She gripped my shoulders, throwing her head back against the window of the door. The blinds moved a bit.

I glanced at them, but from what I could tell, they still blocked out the rest of the world. I didn't pay them any further attention.

I was too lost to think clearly.

Too lost to realize…

That someone was there. Someone was seeing enough to destroy both of us.

"Knox, I can't," Shawn panted. "I can't hold on—"

"Not your job." I found her mouth, got her there, and followed closely behind, my tongue wild, my body completely unleashed.

While. Evil. Watched.

Chapter Thirty-Five

Shawn

"I CAN'T BELIEVE I agreed to this." Knox took a swig from the flask of whiskey that Leo had so graciously prepared while Finn filmed.

"Trust me?" I giggled, holding up the pair of scissors in my hand.

"I think I need more alcohol." Knox stared at the scissors and lifted the flask to his lips again. "Maybe a truck full?"

"It's not like your hair holds power." Leo grinned. "I say we buzz it all off."

Knox actually paled.

"Good idea." I winked at Leo. "But don't worry, Knox. We'll save you a lock to put under your pillow when you cry yourself to sleep."

Finn burst out laughing. "See? This is why I love her."

"Competition," Leo coughed into his hand.

Slater walked in on the chaos and stared. "Why does she

have scissors?"

I snipped the air. "Art project. I'm taking a jackass's hair and taping it to a poster. I'm pretty sure if I tell everyone whose hair it is, I can make at least a grand for books next year."

"Girl has a point." Finn looked impressed.

Slater just narrowed his eyes harder. "You said the only reason you would ever cut your hair…"

The room went silent.

"Who's the unlucky girl?" Slater asked, his eyes finding mine, searching, waiting for me to deny him.

In all honesty, I thought he knew.

The minute Knox had dropped the girlfriend word in class, it had been buzzing around campus. Then again, Slater ignored all gossip and refused to have any sort of social media.

It was weird.

Guys like him…

The good-looking, nice ones, you'd think they'd be all over Instagram, but whenever I mentioned it he became really quiet.

"So, she isn't here to do the honors?" Slater asked the room.

What? Did he want one of us to say it?

"Actually…" I cleared my throat.

"She's my girlfriend." Knox just blurted it out into the universe, as if it was going to lessen the blow as Slater stared him down. "I mean, I like her. I really like her. We're together. Now." Knox always oozed confidence; I had never realized a chink in his armor even existed.

Until now.

When he shifted on his feet.

Slater hung his head and whispered, "You promised."

"This is different."

"Is it, though?"

Finn and Leo wouldn't meet his gaze.

"What am I missing?" I put the scissors back on the table and waited. Nobody would look at me.

Finally, Slater said, "Maybe ask the guys who gangbanged my sister before she overdosed on heroine. Maybe ask her dealer, who's still in this room. Maybe ask the guys who helped end her life. Or maybe, just talk to the guy she was trying to get over the night she took a lethal dose, the guy whose number was labeled *boyfriend* on her phone."

He slammed the door.

Blanketing us in a tense silence.

Nobody spoke.

I could hear my own heart beating.

I tried to convince myself it wasn't true.

But why else would Slater be that angry? That offended at them? What they did for a living? Why else would he...?

"Is that why he quit?"

"Yes," Leo answered. "He didn't want to be associated with 'murderers', his words, not ours."

"And her dealer?"

Finn sighed. "I was dealing on the side. I was a bored rich kid who ran in the wrong circles until these guys. I thought — I thought it would help her anxiety. I gave her Xanax — that's it — but I put her into contact with the guys who could get her heavier stuff. I just didn't know that until it was too late."

I gulped as tears filled my eyes. "And the boyfriend?"

"Me," Knox said in a low voice.

"And all of you... You all—" I couldn't get the words

out.

Leo and Finn eyed each other then Knox.

And then Knox turned around and slammed his hand against my dorm-room door.

Slater answered three slams later with a fist to Knox's jaw.

They stumbled backward against the couch.

I let out a shriek as Finn pulled me out of the way.

"You son of a bitch!" Knox roared. "You had no right!"

"She was my sister!"

"We BROKE UP!"

"Then maybe she wouldn't have killed herself!" Slater bellowed. "She loved you, all three of you! And you led her on, you fed her demons! And it was too much, too much when you guys got your heads on straight, too fucking much—" He punched the wall with his fist, chest heaving. "Never leave a man behind, right? You left her to pick up the pieces, and she was too far gone to even recognize what they fucking looked like."

"I didn't know." Knox's voice cracked. "She pushed me away, pushed all of us away. Leo and Finn thought—" He closed his eyes. "—they thought that if they could just—"

"Replace Knox—" Finn gulped. "—that she'd be okay. She said she just wanted to have fun. We never thought it was that serious until it was too late."

"She overdosed because she couldn't live without you. You guys were like fucking poison to her," Slater said in a quiet voice.

"No, man." Knox grabbed him by the shoulders. "She was poison to herself. Don't you see it? She used us just like she used drugs. Don't you think I asked her to stop? Asked her to get help? How many times do you think I drove her home from parties covered in other guys spit? Seeing her clothes ripped, her face gaunt. She was gone before we even knew it." Then Knox hung his head. "I take full responsibility. I always will. She was calling me for help, and I…" He closed his eyes. "…I ignored it. I couldn't take it anymore."

"She died listening to your voicemail, you fucker!" Slater thundered.

I gasped, covering my mouth with my hands.

Every set of eyes met mine.

Knox's looked pained while the other two just looked guilty. And Slater? He looked like he was visiting hell, and I felt like I was right there with them.

This wasn't about me.

It never had been.

I'd never done drugs.

But I understood what it was like to get addicted to the type of friends these guys were, and knowing I was losing that? It would kill me. And I barely knew them the way she probably had.

I backed up slowly then turned and ran.

Grabbing only my cell phone in the process.

Tears clouded my vision as I took the stairs down to the first floor, and I ran right into Alexa. My cell fell to the ground and shattered.

"Shawn?" Alexa grabbed my hand. "What's wrong? You're shaking!"

"Nothing." I picked up my phone and pressed my free hand to my head. "Sorry, just not the best night I've ever had." I sucked in the tears then lost it as she wrapped her arms around me.

"Shit, what did that guy do to you?"

"Guys, plural. Long story." I sniffed. "I just want to forget about it."

She wrapped an arm around me. "I know just the thing, but we need to get you changed. You can't go to a party dressed like an athlete. Let's get you in a short skirt and party the bad thoughts away. Plus, I heard they have Jell-O shots."

I shrugged. "Count me in."

Chapter Thirty-Six

Knox

"Her cell keeps going to voicemail." I slammed my hand against the couch cushion while Slater tried on his phone.

The minute she'd walked out of the room, I'd punched him, earning a punch back and a black eye.

Leo and Finn had pulled us apart.

And that was when it had hit me.

She hadn't stayed.

I'd scared her away.

I'd done what I knew I would always do.

My past would always be there to haunt the present, and from the look in her eyes, it wasn't something easily forgivable.

I wasn't dumb.

I knew that.

I had just hoped.

That was the fucking problem.

She had me hoping.

And now my chest hurt.

And my brain was overanalyzing every single place she could be and aggressively causing my thoughts to spin out of control. Was she injured? Was she alone? Was she crying?

"Same here," Slater sighed and punched the stupid unicorn.

"Can't believe you still have that thing," I muttered, holding a bag of frozen peas to my face.

Slater shrugged then winced like it hurt to move. "Unicorns were her favorite, and keeping a picture of her just seems... too morbid."

"But keeping a possessed unicorn is what? Better?"

"It's not possessed."

"On multiple occasions, I found it watching me sleep, but sure..."

"Practical joke. She used to—" He smiled then stopped.

"I'm sorry." I didn't know what else to say, and the longer I didn't hear from Shawn the more worried I got. Something didn't feel right.

"Me, too." He stared down at his phone and froze while his entire body went stiff.

"What? She calling?"

My Twitter notification popped up with a picture of Alexa and Shawn with Jessica in the background watching them.

> *Trouble in paradise, @KnoxT. Your girl seems to be partying solo.*

@UWGossip had also been tagged, meaning it had gone to the entire school who followed the stupid feed.

"She's at a party." I stood and tossed the peas on the counter.

Slater kept staring at his phone like he'd seen a ghost.

"I'll find out where and— Are you even listening to me?"

Slater shook his head and, with shaking hands, pulled up the text he'd just received right along with another picture. It was eerily similar, actually taken from the same spot, in that same house, with Jessica in the background, a soft smile on her face.

And Slater's sister with a friend, smiling at the camera.

"What. The. Fuck." Slater was shaking so hard I had to grab his hand to stare at the picture again.

They were identical except for the people front and center.

"It's a sick joke." I gave my head a shake.

"Right." Slater's voice shook. "And if it's not?"

Fear trickled down my spine. "Leo! Finn! Get your asses in here. We're going to a party."

"Do you really think now's the time? I've hacked all the cameras." Finn rubbed his eyes.

I tossed him both our phones.

He looked back and forth between the two of them then ran back into his room. Within seconds, he was back. "It's the sorority Jessica's in."

"It's the same fucking house!" I roared.

Leo was already making his way toward the door.

"We need to call the authorities," I said in a numb voice. "We need to call the police right now."

Chapter Thirty-Seven

Shawn

I KNEW SOMETHING was wrong the minute I had the first sip of my drink, and it wasn't because it tasted funny; it was because Jessica was the one who'd handed it to me. But she was friends with Alexa, not super close, but I figured if Alexa at least trusted her not to poison her, I should too, even though I wanted to rip her black hair from her head.

"Sorry about today." Jessica tapped her cup to mine. "I just— He makes me crazy. It's not you. It's me. Trust me. I used to crush on him really hard, and it kind of sucks being led on for three straight years."

Three. Years.

There it was again.

I tucked my hair behind my ear then took another sip while Alexa left me to dance with some guy in a baseball cap. "Three years?"

She smiled. "Yeah, three long years. He broke up with

his girlfriend then she died in this tragic overdose that kind of shook the school. I mean, you don't expect a girl like that to fall prey to drugs, but I guess it could just happen to anyone."

"You mean she wasn't a druggie?"

"Recreational user." Jessica shrugged. "Like most college kids, her biggest drug was the fact that she had three of the hottest guys on campus panting after her, Knox especially. When that guy falls, he falls so hard he ignores everything around him. Important things."

"Like you?" My eyes narrowed as the room started spinning.

"No, silly." She rolled her eyes. "Like class. I think he almost failed his freshman year because of her."

"Oh." I grabbed her for support when a pretty brunette bumped into me from the side, causing the rest of my drink to fall to the ground.

"Sorry." The girl winked.

"Bitch!" Jessica yelled and steadied me on my feet.

I had beer dripping down the blouse I'd borrowed from Alexa.

"Hey, you all right?"

I briefly saw two of her and slowly shook my head no. "I need… I think I need air or something. I don't feel right. I don't have my… phone…" Wait, what had happened to my phone? It wasn't funny, but I wanted to laugh and cry all at once. And now my clothes were ruined and smelled like beer.

Jessica grabbed my hand. "I'll take you upstairs. You can borrow a shirt before you search for Alexa to take you home."

"Yeah…" I went with her and was suddenly thankful she was stronger than she looked as I leaned on her. The stairs felt taller than normal stairs, my body heavier. Was it the alcohol? I hadn't eaten much that day, and I'd been practicing a lot. I frowned as my brain worked ten times slower than normal.

We walked down the long hall and into Jessica's room. The lights were off and the moment she flicked them on and shut the door behind her, I felt like I was going to puke.

"Oh no, you don't." She shoved me toward the bed. "You puke, and the drugs go out of your system."

"Drugs?" I slurred. "Why are you drugging me? Where's Alexa? Knox!" I started screaming as tears ran down my face.

"Shut up, or I'll make this painful rather than peaceful, bitch." She grabbed something in a bottle then a needle.

My words weren't coming out.

But my mind was moving, calculating.

The overdose.

Knox's name on her phone.

Three. Years.

"You." I stumbled back onto the bed, my body barely moving. Each limb felt too heavy as I tried to get away from her choking presence. "You drugged… her."

Jessica's eyebrows shot up. "Wow, even the police didn't catch that one. Then again, that's the danger in drugs, isn't it? It makes all good girls go bad, and it's so common, you know. Overdoses on college campuses…"

I gagged.

Then tried to put my finger in my mouth. I retched a bit before she could reach me then kicked her in the ribs as hard as I could while I tried to puke more.

"Nice try," she laughed. "It's already in your system. It takes a good solid seven minutes. That's what our story time was about downstairs, you know, though I was a bit worried that you didn't get enough since your drink spilled."

"No." I was so scared I started shaking. This was not how things were supposed to end. I was supposed to have a fresh start. Find someone that saw me, not my skin; find someone who loved me for me. I was supposed to have a life. To graduate.

I saw Knox in that future.

His smile.

I saw my friends Leo, Finn, and Slater.

I saw that stupid bright unicorn.

"You k-killed her." My voice was laced with so much fear that the words came out shaky.

"Hey, she was depressed. All I did was hand her the packed needle. She's the one who shot herself up. I just gave her a little bit too much. How was I supposed to know she'd stop breathing?"

"You'll go to prison." I tried kicking at her again, but my feet were basically lead at that point, my legs weighted with sand as she filled the needle with a substance I didn't want to acknowledge.

As a metallic taste filled my mouth.

As the sound of death rang in my ears, and people all around the house partied like I wasn't fighting for my life.

"Help!" I screeched with the last of my energy. "Help!"

"They didn't hear her. What makes you think they're going to hear you?" Jessica sneered before grabbing a tourniquet and wrapping it around my left arm.

Chapter Thirty-Eight

Knox

I PRAYED WE wouldn't be too late.

I had such a bad feeling, even though I'd called the cops and told them to rush as fast as humanly possible.

Because Jessica had been there in the beginning.

Jessica had been pursuing me before Sophie, during Sophie, after Sophie.

They had been best friends.

I'd held Jessica's hand while she bawled her eyes out at the funeral. I'd held her hand while she spoke in front of the student body about the danger of drug use.

I'd held her body when she decided she needed to use our services to feel better. I'd held her close and hugged her tight when she told me she missed Sophie because she was the only one who'd ever understood her.

I'd held her while she lied.

I had held her.

And even if she hadn't done anything herself, she'd still sat there and watched while her friend had taken a lethal dose of something.

It was too damning.

"Can you drive faster?" I screamed at Leo, who finally pulled up to a nonexistent parking spot.

Slater and I jumped out and started running towards the house.

"Where would she take her?" I asked, searching the crowd for mocha skin as tears pricked the back of my eyes.

Slater searched the room and started asking people where she was, holding a picture of her up on his phone.

I found Alexa dancing with some guy. "Where's Shawn?"

"She went home, bro." The guy dancing with Alexa looked vaguely familiar. Then again, I knew everyone on campus.

Alexa just shrugged, her eyes glassy.

Shit.

I turned and started making my way toward the stairs when my neck prickled with awareness.

I turned to see Slater give me a wide-eyed look like he felt it, too.

It intensified the moment I hit the first stair.

And when I took another, I could smell it.

Smell her.

Sophie.

I ran like hell with Slater behind me.

I kicked open the first two doors with no luck then the third… just in time to see Jessica leaning over Shawn with a needle.

Sirens sounded outside.

Jessica jerked away from Shawn and gave me a saucy

smile. "Almost late to the party. Did you want to do the honors first?"

"I don't do drugs."

"Weird, since your girlfriend clearly does. You think this is my shit? She just wanted to feel better."

"Liar!" Shawn's voice sounded different. "Drugged, she drugged... me... killed... She killed..."

I ran to Shawn's side and pulled her into my arms while she sobbed against my chest.

"You bitch!" Slater roared, charging Jessica. Leo and Finn held him back before he could hit her. "You killed her!"

"Whoa." Jessica dropped the needle on the nightstand and wiped it. "That's a hefty accusation considering her drug use. Don't you think?"

"Drop the act, Jessica," Slater spat. "I know who gave my sister her first hit. I know it was you. Twins, remember? She told me everything. I also knew she was getting clean. We all did! That's why it made no sense!"

Jessica's eyes darted between all of us. "Have fun proving it."

Slater held up his phone. "Oh, I plan on it."

The pictures were side by side, so familiar that a court was going to have a fun time with all the evidence we had, including a testimony from whatever she'd said to Shawn.

The police officers chose that time to make their way down the hall.

"Is this her?" the first one in asked, pointing at Jessica.

"Yes." Slater crossed his arms. "That's the girl who killed my sister three years ago and almost killed my roommate just now."

"You can't prove shit!" she yelled as they cuffed her, read Jessica her rights, and drug her out of the room.

"How'd you… find me?" Shawn sniffed against my chest.

I gave her the only answer that made sense as I locked eyes with Slater. "Sophie showed us."

Chapter Thirty-Nine

Shawn

I COULDN'T STOP shaking.

The drugs had worn off enough for me to talk to the police officers about what had happened. I gave them my statement after the paramedics checked me out to make sure I wasn't dying.

And all the while, Knox held one of my hands while Slater held the other.

Leo and Finn looked as if they were wishing I had more hands to hold, and at one point, I could have sworn each of them looked at a foot and contemplated it. I wasn't sure who needed comforting more.

Me.

Or them.

Because I knew what was going through their heads; it was the same thing going through mine. History repeating itself. Their faults.

Their business.

The death of Slater's sister.

And all the things in between because of one girl's hate.

But sadly, that was the world we lived in. Hate for someone's religion, someone's skin color, someone's sexual orientation. Everywhere I looked, I saw hate.

And it was damn time for it to stop.

I was done.

So done.

I glanced across the street to see Jessica sitting in a cop car, tears streaming down her face as if she was just now realizing what she had done and what she had been about to do.

I would be one less human full of hate.

Tonight, I would be one less.

I let go of Knox's hand and jumped off the back of the ambulance, a bit unsteady on my feet. Slater tried to hold on, but I let go. I walked by Leo and Finn, felt them all follow me as I made my way to the cop car with the flashing lights and the hateful person inside.

The window was down.

"What!" she yelled through her tears. "You know my lawyer is going to—"

"I'm sorry." I put my hand on the windowsill. "I'm sorry you're hurting. I'm sorry that you felt you had to hurt others in order to feel better. And I just want you to know... I forgive you."

She looked away. "I don't need your forgiveness."

"I know. But you get it anyway."

"Ma'am..." The police officer I'd talked to, the one with the easy smile and bushy eyebrows approached. "...would you like to press charges?"

I wanted to.

I wanted to strangle her.

I felt so many things for the girl who'd tried to take my life away from me.

Who had succeeded in taking it away from Slater's sister, Sophie.

But hate plus hate did not equal love.

"No," I finally said. "I don't want to press charges. I want her to get help."

"A restraining order," Knox piped up. "Is that up for discussion?"

"Doesn't matter," the officer sighed. "We found evidence of drug possession in her room, along with multiple accounts of usage and selling for personal gain, not to mention the damning evidence in Sophie Jackson's case. I don't imagine she's going to be getting community service. She's going to be tried for first-degree murder."

I wasn't sure if Jessica had heard all of that.

But I knew the laws.

If you sell someone something, and they overdose on it...

You get tried for first-degree murder.

And I wasn't sorry that she was dealing with the consequences. I just knew it wasn't my job to add more sentences on top of what she was already dealing with.

Besides, if I didn't put a stop to the hate, who would?

It was each of us...

Individually making a choice to forgive, rather than condemn.

So, I held my head high the entire way home in Knox's car, and when I felt like puking out of fear, I gripped his hand tighter and remembered that I wasn't alone.

And would never be again.

Chapter Forty

Knox

She'd wanted to shower.

And I'd refused to let her go.

The guys must have felt the same because when she announced what she was doing, we all waited for her to grab her shower caddy. Leo took it from her, Finn grabbed a towel, Slater started making her food, and I carried her to the first shower stall and started the hot water.

"Hey!" Leo complained, "That's my job. Make the water hot…"

Shawn gave him a shaky smile then burst into a mess of tears and hiccups as I set her on her feet and pulled her close.

And when Leo and Finn joined us in a group hug…

It wasn't weird.

None of it was weird.

It was right.

As if we needed that moment to know that we'd done

it — that she was alive and okay in our arms.

Leo first kissed the top of her head, followed by Finn. They walked out, leaving me with the girl I'd almost lost. "What would I have done?" my voice cracked. "Your warm skin? Your smile… your hair…" I felt my eyes well with tears. "I don't want to be in a world where you don't exist, where your smile isn't lighting up every room we're in. That's not a happy world, Shawn."

"I'm so sorry," she cried against my chest.

"This isn't your fault!" I gripped her chin and lifted so I could gaze into her eyes. "Look at me. This isn't your fault! It's ours! Had we known—"

"Hard to know a psychopath is coming after you when she smiles while holding a drink in one hand and a needle in the other."

"I'm sorry." I kissed her eyes. "So fucking sorry. What can I do? I'll do anything to make you feel safe again — anything."

"Anything?" She pulled away.

"Yeah."

"Just help me get the smell of the party off of me, get me out of these clothes. I just… I just want to feel safe."

"I swear I'll always keep you safe." I meant it.

"I know." Her smile was small, hopeful, as I slowly unzipped her skirt until it fell to the tile floor. I unbuttoned the blouse and tossed it. They were going in the trash, along with every other thing she was wearing. Her panties and her bra followed, though the pretty pale pink against her skin was just another reminder of what she had been wearing the day she could have died.

I gathered them all in a pile and shoved them in the trash then came back and started peeling off my clothes.

Her eyes widened. "You're joining me?"

"Yup." I shoved down my jeans. "The way I see it, I'm now your personal bodyguard. Hope you don't mind, but I'm probably not going to let you pee without asking if you're okay."

This time she laughed. It wasn't the same as her normal laugh, but it was something. "You know she's in jail right now, right? She can't hurt me."

"Then let me protect you from everyone else who's stupid enough to try."

She smiled. "I can't really argue that logic, can I?"

"Nope." I tested the water then helped her into the shower and followed. Once the hot stream flowed over our bodies, she got busy scrubbing her skin clean, and I tried... I tried like hell not to watch the soap glide across her mocha flesh, just like I tried not to focus on the way her breasts bounced with each movement of her arms.

At one point, I even turned around and scolded my own body for not getting the point that she'd just been scared for her life, while there I was, ready to take her against the shower wall.

With sheer willpower, I helped her rinse then wrapped a towel around her shivering body before grabbing one for me. I dried off, put on my clothes then carried her into the joint suite, still in her towel since I'd dumped her clothes.

"Look, Finn. Knox brought us a Christmas goose." Leo winked. "All pink and ready to eat."

Slater groaned. "I'm fixing food, try not to make everything sexual."

Leo smirked while Finn just shook his head.

I carried Shawn into her bedroom, shut the door, and started rummaging through her drawers.

"Hey, I can do it." Her hand met mine as soon as I collided with a lacy black thong. "Especially if that's what you're picking for comfort right now."

I dropped it as if it was burning my skin while she chose a pair of boy shorts, which actually made me harder than when I was touching the thong, then grabbed a tank top and pulled it right over her wet head.

I cleared my throat. "We should get you a bra."

"Should we?" She looked down.

I let out a groan. "Yeah, we really should."

She went to the door.

"Shawn—"

She turned the lock then faced me. "I want you."

"Everyone's waiting outside. They're all concerned—"

She only took one step before I pulled her in my arms then shrugged out of my own shirt while trying to peel hers over her head.

She was in her white boy shorts; me in my jeans again.

I could taste her fear, her desire to force it away.

So, I promised I would take it. Promised that if she didn't feel safe in this world anymore, she'd at least always feel safe in my arms.

"We don't have to do this." I gripped her by the elbows and searched her eyes, not for an excuse to pull away, but for a reason to stay, a reason to feel okay about this moment.

"Knox…" She breathed my name against my lips.

I could taste her. I could feel her pulse.

"…let me need you."

What more could a broken man ask for?

Than to be needed.

By someone like her.

I kissed her hard and dove my hands into her hair while

she swirled her tongue around mine like she was trying to taste every angle. The sweet smell of her soap filled the room as I tugged her underwear down with my fingers over her clean skin, past her thighs, past her knees. She kicked them away as we stumbled to her small twin bed.

I drew out the kisses longer and deeper until I noticed the red skin around her mouth from my scruff. I didn't care. I wanted to mark her. Wanted the guys to see that she was mine. She would always and forever be mine.

My body flexed over her as I pulled my jeans off and discarded them on the floor. I crawled onto the bed and felt too protective of this girl.

"You're so brave." I tucked her hair behind her ears and nuzzled her neck. "So fucking brave."

"I'm not," she said through tears. "I was so scared, and I felt so stupid that in those last few seconds when she was holding the needle close to my skin, I just… I thought of what could have been."

"We don't have to talk about it."

"But we do…" Shawn gripped my neck and pulled me closer. "…because all I saw was you. All I see is you. Us. And for a few seconds, I felt fine, because I saw you."

Tears filled my eyes. "I don't deserve your final seconds."

"And what about the next few minutes? Hours? Days? Months? What about now, Knox?"

Her breath hitched as I ran my hands up her ribs, touching her skin, causing goose bumps to erupt all over the most gorgeous brown I'd ever seen. "Now, we can stop counting."

"Because you can't count that high?" she teased.

I laughed because her comment was so unexpected.

And when she joined in, I breathed a sigh of relief.

A shiver ran down her body as I kissed her again. I rubbed the slim dip above her hip and kissed her there too. And when I saw the mark from the tourniquet on her arm, I kissed that.

Her eyes glimmered as our mouths met again, slow and fast, fast and slow. No more words were really needed as I urged her forward, first with my fingertips then with my tongue, as I tasted her on my lips and made sure she knew that this was more.

It would always be more.

Her eyes fluttered open when I pulled her to a sitting position, laid down on my back then tugged her on top of me.

I held her breasts, squeezed as she eased onto me and took control. I gave it to her the way she needed it on a day when all control had been lost.

With each thrust into her body, I knew I wouldn't last long. I'd almost lost her. I just wanted to claim her again. Every dormant part of my body that had been shut off to this emotion awakened.

She was mine.

Her lips quivered with passion as she gripped my hand and pressed it against the pillow, her body moving faster. I held on to her until I felt her muscles tense. Until the searing heat between us exploded. Her spasms hit me so hard and fast that I went over the edge with her.

She fell against my chest, and wet tears slid down my skin. "Thank you for saving me."

"I didn't save you. You… saved me. Actually, you saved us." Her body felt heavy against mine.

An hour later, I snuck out and told the guys she'd crashed. The food had grown cold. Slater returned to the room, but the scowl on his face was replaced with relief as he watched her slow, even breathing.

"I just can't b-believe it," his voice cracked. "I blamed you so much. I—"

"I blamed myself too. I still do. We still went wrong in so many ways, man. I think I need to contact Wingman and let them know that freshmen are too immature to take on clients. We'll train them and wait until they're juniors. It was like a God-complex, knowing people would pay just to be with us, and while we made a shit-ton of money, the lines were too blurred for eighteen-year-old horny guys… and I don't think Wingman ever took into consideration the jealousy of other clients."

"Yeah," he croaked.

A chill hit the room.

I pointed. "Did you leave the window open?"

"Dude, you know these windows don't open." Slater frowned just as something crunched under his foot. With shaking hands, he picked it up from the floor. It was a picture of him and Sophie, one that hadn't been there before.

I grinned. "She looks so happy with you here."

"Yeah, and I look like I'm sexually confused standing with that stupid unicorn I won her at the fair."

"She didn't choose to leave this life, man." I put my hand on his back. "Maybe it's time we all moved past it and remembered her for the good, not the bad."

"Yeah. Thanks for…" He swallowed hard. "…just thanks."

I moved to grab the door when Shawn moaned in her sleep, "Stay."

Slater rolled his eyes. "Just make sure I'm out of the room when you start doing all the touching."

I laughed. "I promise."

Chapter Forty-One

Shawn

I WOKE UP to moaning.

Not the kind I was trying to get used to, more the irritated kind. It was enough to make me curious. Besides, Slater wasn't in bed, Knox had left at some point, and the unicorn was creepily staring at me from the foot of my bed like some weird guard dog with pink hair.

I yawned, put on some sweats, and opened the door.

The sound of moaning suddenly made sense.

I almost wished it had been the sexual kind.

"Put your back into it!" Leo moaned again. "Yeah, just like that. That's the spot."

"You tell anyone I touched you, I'm killing you." Slater massaged his foot harder. "And this is bullshit. You know it is."

"Ah, the rules clearly state if you want back in, you gotta prove that you haven't lost all your talent." He sighed. "My other foot has a fungus. Try to be gentle."

Slater jerked away.

"I'm kidding!" Leo laughed. "But seriously, if I did have a fungus, you'd have to just go with the flow and pretend it was a flower growing on my big toe."

Finn frowned. "Did you just rhyme about fungus?"

"Flowers," Knox corrected, flipping a pancake then stirring some sausage.

I cleared my throat.

And suddenly, four guys were stumbling toward me. Finn pulled me in for a hug then told me my hair looked pretty. Liar.

Leo started rubbing my shoulders while Slater grabbed a blanket and sat me on the couch. He handed me a fresh cup of coffee. And then there was Knox.

Shirtless Knox.

With. Short. Hair.

I covered my mouth with my hands and spoke through my fingers, "You cut your hair!"

He shrugged. "I'm a taken man. Don't need that Samson hair hanging around when I have you."

"But the good version of you, not the Bible's version of a man-hater," Finn said with a grin.

I ran my fingers through the strands; it still hung to his ears, and it made him look even more attractive, which just irritated me more.

He smiled and leaned in, kissing my neck. "I made you food."

"We all made you food," Leo corrected.

"And Slater? Why's he training?"

"Oh, he swallowed his pride, shotgunned two beers, and is re-training so he can be part of the… What did you call it, bro?" Finn crossed his arms.

Slater gritted his teeth. "Pleasure Ponies."

I burst out laughing, feeling a bit more like myself. "Catchy, right?" I took a bite out of the pancakes. "And why is Slater joining the, uh, force?"

"I resigned," Knox said with a shrug of his shoulders. "Something about cutting my hair and claiming the most beautiful woman in the world kind of makes doing favors sound like the worst possible choice I could make."

"I wouldn't have made you quit," I said softly.

"Well, I talked with Wingman, Inc. today. Ian wasn't super happy that we were down to two — especially since this year was the highest grossing year of usage they'd seen with the new app — so Slater, eavesdropping bastard, said he'd take my place. And here we are." He smiled.

"Bitch..." Leo pointed to his foot. "...you think you're done here?"

"Shit, I'm regretting that decision." Slater sat and grabbed Leo's foot. "For the record, I know how to do your jobs just as good as you do."

"Prove it," Leo challenged.

Slater moved a hand to the back of my neck, hit a spot that gave me chills, and all eyes fell to my chest.

I crossed my arms and glared.

Knox smacked Slater on the back of the head. "Do that again, and I'm throwing you out the window."

"And the gang's all back together," Finn chuckled darkly. "Oh, and that's the spot for arousal, not chills, but she has Knox so..."

I gulped and tried to act normal when my body suddenly felt heavy, my thighs tingly.

Knox dropped the pancakes onto the table and winked

at Slater. "Thanks, man."

I barely had a chance to say anything when his lips were plastered to mine, and we were back inside my room.

"Is that real?" I asked between kisses and breaths. "The whole arousal thing?"

"Who the fuck cares?" He pulled my shirt off and kissed me harder.

I laughed against his kiss as we stumbled toward the bed, clothes flying. It wasn't until he was naked, pressed against me, holding me in the middle of the room that I saw the picture of Slater, his arm wrapped around a beautiful girl with big eyes and an even bigger smile.

"Who's that in the picture with Slater?"

"His sister, Sophie." He kissed my head. "Why?"

"She was at the party. She — she stumbled into me. I spilled almost my entire drink, the one Jessica had drugged—" I shook my head. "You know what? Never mind…" I kept the thoughts to myself.

Because in a weird way, it made sense.

I turned around in his arms.

I kissed him for her.

I kept him for me.

Epilogue

Knox

"You did good." Ian sat back against the giant-ass desk in his downtown Seattle office building. Wingman, Inc. was doing well. They didn't just own floor space; they owned the entire damn building.

"Thanks." I leaned forward and clasped my hands together. "I'm glad Slater worked out for the last half of the semester."

Ian tilted his head. "And things between you guys... Are they better?"

"Is this therapy?"

"Cocky little shit. Why do you think I hired you?"

"Because I'm better looking?" I heard a laugh behind me as Lex, his business partner, walked in and took a long sip of his coffee.

"Oh, don't mind me." Lex held up his hands in innocence. "I was just enjoying my eavesdropping." He sat on the park bench that Ian kept on one side of the office. Rumor had it that was where Wingmen, Inc. had been born, but how was I supposed to know?

Ian cleared his throat. "You earned your position with us, but don't get too comfortable. I can still fire your ass."

"Noted." I stood and held out my hand.

He gripped it and smiled. "VP of Marketing and Development. How's it feel?"

"It feels like I should get a bonus." I pulled him in for a hug.

"You're lucky we're related, cousin. And you're lucky that the apple didn't fall far from the tree…" He sighed. "Fifty."

"Dollars?"

Lex choked on a laugh again.

"Thousand," Ian clarified with a grin. "Signing bonus, and for putting up with my shit for four entire years. I have all the paperwork ready to go. You start Monday. Oh, and family dinner tonight."

"Wow, it's like you're finally letting me in the inner circle."

Lex stood and gave me a pat on the back. "Circle? Yes. Inner sanctum? Hell no."

"Thanks." I shook his hand too and grabbed the portfolio from Ian's hands then turned around and walked out the door toward my future.

And the waiting girl talking with Ian's and Lex's wives outside.

Shawn's hands were animated as she started telling Blake a story then Finn and Leo walked up with Slater and put their arms around all the girls.

"One…" I whispered. "Two—"

"Get your hands off my wife!" Ian shouted from the

office.

Leo and Finn didn't listen. Then again, they looked at Ian as more of a friend than anything. He was the one who'd seen our potential and given us jobs, and the story didn't end there.

After all, they still had one more year left with Slater.

While I was mentally preparing for my future.

My future with Shawn.

And whatever else that meant as long as she was by my side.

"Hey..." I pulled her into my arms and kissed her on the mouth. "You ready to go celebrate?"

"Are you ready?" she countered with a smirk.

"What's that? That smile you have right now?"

"We're all going to Dave and Busters!" she announced proudly.

"YES!" Slater jumped into the air.

I hung my head. "Last time we almost got kicked out."

"Because..." Shawn tugged my hands. "...you got too upset and threw a basketball at Finn's face."

"Finn was cheating," I pointed out. I would have yelled, but this was my new workplace, and I was about to take on the role of boss to some of these people. "Besides, why are we going there for my celebration dinner?"

"Finn promised to play fair," Shawn pointed out. "And I want a rematch. Remember what happened last time you won?"

I grinned so hard my face hurt. "So, if I win again..."

"Exactly." She wrapped her arms around my neck then whispered against my ear, "Don't you want to play?"

I swallowed my excitement and kissed her instead. "Oh, I'll play."

"Thought so." She winked. "See? So, it really is the best place to celebrate."

"Yeah." I grabbed her hand as we waved goodbye and made our way to the elevator. "It really is."

If you or someone you know is struggling with addiction there is help, you aren't alone.

SAMHSA's National Helpline:
https://www.samhsa.gov/find-help/national-helpline

Wingmen Inc

Can't get enough of the WINGMEN?
See where it all started!

The Matchmaker's Playbook

Wingman rule number one: don't fall for a client.

After a career-ending accident, former NFL recruit Ian Hunter is back on campus—and he's ready to get his new game on. As one of the masterminds behind Wingmen, Inc., a successful and secretive word-of-mouth dating service, he's putting his extensive skills with women to work for the lovelorn. But when Blake Olson requests the services of Wingmen, Inc., Ian may have landed his most hopeless client yet.

From her frumpy athletic gear to her unfortunate choice of footwear, Blake is going to need a miracle if she wants to land her crush. At least with a professional matchmaker by her side she has a fighting chance. Ian knows that his advice and a makeover can turn Blake into another successful match. But as Blake begins the transformation from hot mess to smokin' hot, Ian realizes he's in danger of breaking his cardinal rule…

Free on Kindle Unlimited
Purchase: http://bit.ly/RVDPlaybook

NOW STREAMING ON PASSIONFLIX!
Subscribe to Passionflix: http://bit.ly/RVDPassionflix

The Matchmaker's Replacement

Wingman rule number two: never reveal how much you want them.

Lex hates Gabi. Gabi hates Lex. But, hey, at least the hate is mutual, right? All Lex has to do is survive the next few weeks training Gabi in all the ways of Wingmen Inc. and then he can be done with her. But now that they have to work together, the sexual tension and fighting is off the charts. He isn't sure if he wants to strangle her or throw her against the nearest sturdy table and have his way with her.

But Gabi has a secret, something she's keeping from not just her best friend but her nemesis too. Lines are blurred as Lex becomes less the villain she's always painted him to be… and starts turning into something more. Gabi has always hated the way she's been just a little bit attracted to him— no computer-science major should have that nice of a body or look that good in glasses—but "Lex Luthor" is an evil womanizer. He's dangerous. Gabi should stay far, far away.

Then again, she's always wanted a little danger.

Free on Kindle Unlimited
Purchase: http://bit.ly/RVDReplacement

COMING SOON TO PASSIONFLIX!

Dirty Exes

About the Book

They're serving up some red-hot revenge. A sizzling series from #1 *New York Times* bestselling author Rachel Van Dyken.

Blaire has never quite gotten over Jessie Beckett, the ex–NFL star whose kisses were hot enough to ignite the entire Eastern Seaboard. When he chose work over her, Blaire was left brokenhearted. Why else would she have married a skeezy two-timer, just to divorce him less than a year later?

Now Blaire is getting even by becoming one half of Dirty Exes, a PI firm fully committed to humiliating cheating jerks. If only the new jerk she's been hired to uncover wasn't Jessie Beckett himself.

Exposing Jessie isn't going to be easy, especially when she still daydreams about his sexy smile. Further complicating matters is Colin, Jessie's best friend. He's gorgeous, a little bit cunning, and willing to help Blaire get the inside scoop on Jessie—for a price.

Now caught between two men—one *totally right* and the other *totally wrong*—Blaire will need to decide just how much she's willing to risk…and whom she's willing to risk it for.

Releasing June 5!
Pre-Order here: http://bit.ly/RVDDirtyExes

Excerpt

"Bingo," I whispered and quickly plugged in my fiber-optic camera. God bless iPhones and all the little gadgets that come with them. As quietly as possible, I climbed the ladder and shoved the camera up through the gritty metal hole.

"Come to mama," I whispered as my adrenaline spiked.

Isla said she'd lure him out of the restaurant with the promise of a quickie, and the cheating idiot—the one who really needed to learn how to shop in his own garage, if you get my meaning—was clearly all over it. What was it with men who thought that money made up for their overactive sweat glands and jowls the size of my ass?

"God, you're a beautiful woman," lying, cheating bastard crooned in a gravelly voice that reminded me of those antismoking commercials. My face twisted with disgust while I recorded. The angle was perfect, and the street lights may as well have been spotlights on his eager face.

"Awww." My best friend and business partner shrugged a shoulder and forced a laugh. She tugged down the front of her dress, and the cheater took one look at her breasts and made a choking noise. Apparently he had an overactive salivary gland too. "You're such a nice guy. How are you not married?"

"Just haven't found the right woman, I suppose." He

toyed with the black material near her right nipple, flicking it with his swollen and heavily ringed pointer finger. I kept myself from throwing up.

"Is that so?" She leaned in. "How is that even possible?"

"No idea." He leaned in.

Oh, honey, I appreciate the dedication but he probably tastes like an ashtray. Don't do it, don't do it. I briefly contemplated closing my eyes so I wouldn't have to witness any forthcoming kiss. Only a best friend would notice the slight grimace Isla made before backing up and sliding a manila envelope out of her bag and shoving it into his chest.

"What's this?" He chuckled at the envelope while she made a gagging noise and wiped her mouth. The guy hadn't even kissed her, yet her body was in distress, poor thing.

"You got it?" She looked down at the sewer cover.

I moved the fiber-optic cable up and down in an affirmative motion.

She smirked at him. "You've just been served. You're also on camera, so say hi to your wife and the rest of the Dirty Exes, our live Facebook group. And while you're at it, you may as well say goodbye to half of everything you own according to the prenup you signed three years ago. But you know what? Half doesn't seem nearly enough to put up with your shit."

I cackled.

His phone buzzed.

"Better answer that, I'm pretty sure that's your soon-to-be-ex-wife just making sure you're aware that she saw the live video." She smiled triumphantly. "Oh, and nice doing business with you."

With great effort, I removed the sewer lid then heaved myself up the rest of the way. The cover felt like it weighed twenty-five pounds, and I nearly smashed my fingers in the name of catching another cheater. I'd do it again in a heartbeat.

"You smell." Isla scrunched up her nose when she waltzed over to me. "But you're dedicated, I like it."

"It was the only way to get close enough," I grumbled and made an effort to dust off my damp clothes even though I knew it was in vain. When she'd texted she'd be meeting the target, I'd been headed back to my apartment, so I was ill prepared for sewer sightseeing even though I knew it was a possibility, considering the location. Can one ever be completely prepared to do something like that? The answer is no. Just. No.

"You bitches!" The Cheater ran toward both of us—lips curled in disgust, his eyes beady, angry little lasers, hand raised—like he was seconds away from attacking us with his cell phone.

Instinctively, I reared back and let my fist fly. Knuckles connected with flesh, and he whimpered and went down like the loser he was.

"Blaire!" Isla groaned. "You can't just punch our clients' husbands."

"I slipped," I lied. "Besides, it was self-defense! He's twice my size and he made a threat!"

Isla just shook her head at me.

"He charged us! With his phone! That's not normal behavior, plus it looked like he intended to use it as a weapon."

I may have anger issues.

"Who the hell are you people?" Cheater was on the ground, covering his face with his hands. Oh hell, was he crying?

I stepped over his sad, pathetic body and grinned. "The Exes."

Isla looped her arm through mine and then dropped our black-and-white calling card on the ground. It was our final punch to the gut. Not only did it serve to warn our targets that we were watching . . . always watching, future clients who randomly found our cards called us based on curiosity alone. We grew our social media presence by being selective and only taking high-profile clients. Business was booming.

"Have a good night." I waved and shoved my phone back in my pocket.

Isla sucked in a breath. "So, pizza?"

"Fries," I countered.

"Pizza." She narrowed her eyes like she was thinking.

"Wine," we said in unison.

"Oh, lookee here." She pulled a bottle out of her giant Mary Poppins purse and waved it in front of my face like it was totally legal to drink while walking down the street.

"You have glasses in there too?" I laughed, poking my head in her giant bag.

She was already pulling them out.

Of course.

Always prepared, Isla was.

"And a screw top." I pointed. "Best date of my life."

"Isn't it though?"

"She'll get more than half." I nodded as Isla poured my red Solo cup to the rim. "You know you didn't have to seduce him, he was well on his way to dropping trousers near the dumpster."

"Our clients expect dedication. Yours was the sewer, mine was his mouth and body." She scrunched up her nose. "Same thing, different locations."

I shuddered. "So true."

Isla stopped walking and lifted her cup in the air. "To another successful divorce."

I clinked my cup with hers. "Men. Women. People of LA, you've been warned: the Exes are here, so keep it in your pants—"

"Or panties!" Isla giggled.

I tilted my head and continued, "Or get it chopped off." I scrunched up my nose. "Too far?"

She hesitated and then tilted her head. "I was thinking more along the lines of running all male penises over with a car, but most are so small I was having trouble figuring out the specifics."

I doubled over in laughter. "Yeah, I'll drink to that. And don't worry, I'm sure the longer we do this the more creative your imagination will get."

A couple passed us by. As I watched them kiss, I ignored the pang in my heart.

Just like I ignored the longing that came with it.

Stupid heart.

"You're happy, right?" Isla asked. She was my other half. If the other half oozed sexuality and confidence. Most days I was lucky I even put on mascara and remembered to wash my hair. I was so focused on retribution, on not focusing on the past, that I was barely staying sane. I wanted to be that woman, the one who told the world where to stick it—I just didn't know how to do it without acknowledging all the parts of myself that were still broken, still hurting. Because that meant I had to actually admit it happened, it was real, and I was alone.

An impasse, that's where I was at.

"Of course!" I said loudly, realizing she was waiting for

my response, and like an idiot I was peering into my wine cup like it was a magic 8 ball that would give me all life's secrets if I just stared hard enough. Her eyebrow arched, and I could tell she wasn't convinced. I took a deep breath, forced a soft smile, and said it again. "I'm really, really happy."

I just had to repeat it.

And then add in two reallys.

She gave me a confident nod and wrapped her arm around me. "Good."

And that was it.

Except it wasn't.

Because a part of me was still thinking about that couple, about the look in her eyes when he kissed her, and about the way it felt to be kissed.

A really good kiss.

One that stunned you into silence. One that stole your breath and made you swear that if you died in that minute, it would be okay. A kiss that made you believe that maybe, just maybe, the world wasn't all bad.

That maybe love existed.

It was that kind of kiss.

And I realized in that moment, with a jarring sense of insecurity, that I'd only ever been kissed like that once in my entire life.

And it wasn't my ex-husband who had done it.

Releasing June 5!
Pre-Order here: http://bit.ly/RVDDirtyExes

Acknowledgements

I SAY THIS every time. Because it's true every time, maybe as I get older I'm realizing it more and more, just what an amazing Gift from God to be able to do what you love day in and day out. To be able to interact with people all over the world. To have this opportunity to create worlds and characters is something that I'm so thankful for. I thank God every day and I'm so thankful to the readers, bloggers, humans in the world that read my books and support me. Thank you from the bottom of my heart. I always miss people when I say thank you. Mainly because it takes a HUGE community of bloggers, publicists, agents, publishers, marketers, etc to get a book born and shipped out into the world.

Thank you to Nina, Jill, Becca, Ang, and Jena. The amazing team behind all the things that go on! I would be lost without you guys, quite literally, we all know that's what happens every time I go to New York, someone has to babysit because streets confuse me and when you can't see the sky…

well HOW DO YOU KNOW WHERE YOU ARE? And I only got lost that one time on that fifty-two block walk to the 9-11 museum. Worth it.

Thank you to my group Rachel's Rockin' Readers, man what an amazing and sane place to be! I love you guys so hard, thank you to my moderators in there who keep things classy and thank you to the readers and authors that make up one of the most positive groups on Facebook. I love you all so much!

To Social Butterfly PR and the bloggers on this tour, thank you for taking a chance on something different! To Give Me Books who always do such an amazing job partnering with us!

And of course, my amazing agent Erica thanks for doing all the things and making sure I stay sane!

My beta readers help SO MUCH and they were pivotal with this book, Tracey, Krista, Liza, Stephanie, Jill, and Jessica. Thanks for reading and giving me your honest feedback, I so need it! And you're never afraid to call me out when I need it, which is on a daily basis!

To my amazing husband and son, you guys are my world. I would be lost without you.

If you guys want to follow my writing journey just hop on Facebook and type in my name or my group Rachel's New Rockin Readers, or find me on insta/twitter @RachVD, hugs! Until next time! RVD

About The Author

RACHEL VAN DYKEN is a *New York Times, Wall Street Journal,* and *USA Today* bestselling author. When she's not writing about hot hunks for her Regency romance or New Adult fiction books, Rachel is dreaming up *new* hunks. (The more hunks, the merrier!) While Rachel writes a lot, she also makes sure she enjoys the finer things in life — like *The Bachelor* and strong coffee.

Rachel lives in Idaho with her husband, son, and two boxers. Fans can follow her writing journey at www.RachelVanDykenAuthor.com and www.facebook.com/rachelvandyken.

Also By Rachel Van Dyken

Seaside Series
Tear
Pull
Shatter
Forever
Fall
Strung
Eternal

Seaside Pictures
Capture
Keep
Steal

Waltzing With The Wallflower
Waltzing with the Wallflower
Beguiling Bridget
Taming Wilde

London Fairy Tales
Upon a Midnight Dream
Whispered Music
The Wolf's Pursuit
When Ash Falls

Renwick House
The Ugly Duckling Debutante
The Seduction of Sebastian St. James
The Redemption of Lord Rawlings
An Unlikely Alliance
The Devil Duke Takes a Bride

Ruin Series
Ruin
Toxic
Fearless
Shame

The Consequence Series
The Consequence of Loving Colton
The Consequence of Revenge
The Consequence of Seduction
The Consequence of Rejection

The Dark Ones Series
The Dark Ones
Untouchable Darkness
Dark Surrender
Darkest Temptation

Wingmen Inc.
The Matchmaker's Playbook
The Matchmaker's Replacement

The Bachelors of Arizona
The Bachelor Auction
The Playboy Bachelor
The Bachelor Contract

Curious Liaisons
Cheater
Cheater's Regret

Players Game
Fraternize
Infraction

Other Titles
The Parting Gift
Compromising Kessen
Savage Winter
Divine Uprising
Every Girl Does It
RIP
Co-Ed

RACHEL VAN DYKEN BOOKS

www.rachelvandykenauthor.com

CPSIA information can be obtained
at www.ICGtesting.com
Printed in the USA
LVOW10s1449010518
575552LV00015B/238/P